Praise for *After the Sun*

"Eika's prose flexes a light-footed, vigilant, and unpredictable animalism: it's practically pantheresque. *After the Sun* is an electrifying, utterly original read."
– Claire-Louise Bennett, author of *Pond*

"Political fictions aren't supposed to be this personal. Satires aren't supposed to be this heartbreaking. Surrealism isn't supposed to be this real. Giving a damn isn't supposed to be this fun. From slights of hand, to shocks to the heart, *After the Sun* is doing all the things you don't expect it to and leaving a big bold mark in what we call literature."
– Marlon James, author of *Black Leopard, Red Wolf*

"Striking literary craftsmanship in an experimental mix of shock-lit, sci-fi, dada and Joycean glints presented as loose time scenes that slide in and out like cards in the hands of the shuffler. By the end, this reader had the impression of having been drawn through a keyhole."
– Annie Proulx, author of *Barkskins*

"Jonas Eika blew the doors and windows of my imagination open, and now there is a galaxy in my head and a supernova in my heart. *After the Sun* vibrates with the aftershock of capitalism and reality flux. Its characters confront the world we've made as if they are facing off with ex-lovers who won't leave, caught at the instant before they will either flame on or flame out. Thrilling."
– Lidia Yuknavitch, author of *The Chronology of Water*

"An urgent, deliriously discomforting reflection of how we're all con-nected with one another — and what it is we expect in exchange for that kind of access. Eika holds nothing back in his fiction, he goes into the tightest of spaces and most intimate and terrifying of moments in order to break through to places few have been before — or even imagined existing."
– *Refinery29*

After the Sun

Jonas Eika

Translated by
Sherilyn Nicolette Hellberg

Lolli Editions
London

Contents

Alvin 11

Bad Mexican Dog 37

Rachel, Nevada 57

Me, Rory and Aurora 89

Bad Mexican Dog 117

Alvin

I arrived in Copenhagen sweaty and halfway out of myself after an extremely fictional flight. Frankly, I would use that word for any air travel, but on this trip I had, shortly after take-off, fallen into a light feverish daze in which I relived a series of flights I had taken earlier in my life. First, there was the trip home from Nepal with my ex-wife, then-girlfriend, our first trip together, when we, maybe out of boredom, curled up in our seats and took turns miming various sexual scenarios that the other person had to guess and sketch on a piece of paper, which we tore into pieces and reassembled into new situations to mime again, so that the game could continue for eternities. In my daze there was also my departure from Copenhagen six years later, after she became pregnant around the same time that she had been cheating on me with a colleague, and I was so panicked and grieved by my jealousy — which seemed just as impossible to live with if the baby was mine as if it wasn't — that I packed my things, went to the airport and said Málaga to the man behind the counter, for some reason I said Málaga. Additionally, I relived a flight home from a work trip a few years later, during which I was unable to work, to say a word to anyone, because I was completely paralysed by what I had seen from my window during take-off: Past the gates, overlooking the runway, there was an observation deck where kids of all ages stood with their parents watching the planes take off. At one corner, a woman stood with her back to the railing — long, dark hair in the frozen sun — looking at a man running toward her, across the deck, and as we flew past he fell to the ground as if shot by a gun. I couldn't hear the gunshot, if one had even been fired, and the plane continued into the clouds with me sitting stiff in my seat for the rest of the flight, doubting what I had seen. What was uncomfortable, feverish, about the stupor in which I re-experienced these flights, was how it slid across the surface of sleep as if over a low-pressure area, into a zone in which I was vaguely aware of the *original* flight, the one I was on now, which for that reason was hidden somewhere underneath or behind: *the cabin* hidden behind, *the food cart*, *my fellow passengers* and *the clouds outside the window* hidden behind these past, recalled and also in that sense extremely fictional flights. I felt a hand on my shoulder and opened my eyes to a single-faced flight attendant. Everyone else had already left the plane. The cabin was quiet and empty. On the way out, I looked at the windows and the carpet, the overhead luggage compartments and emergency-exit signs, and I ran my fingers along the thick stitches in the leather seats.

At passport control, I passed quickly through the entrance for EU citizens. I took the metro to Kongens Nytorv and hurried to the bank's headquarters to make it in time for my meeting with the system administrator that afternoon. As I turned the corner, I smelled something mouldy and burnt, a mix of fire and vegetable rot, and when I saw the red-and-white police tape, I started walking faster. The building had collapsed and tall piles of marble, steel, pale wood and office furniture lay dispersed among other unidentifiable materials. Beneath the scraps I could make out the edge of a pit, places where the earth slanted steeply into itself in the way that lips sometimes slant into the mouths of old people. Three or four servers protruded between the floorboards and whiteboards; funny, I thought, since the floors had just been elevated in anticipation of rising sea levels. A police officer told me that the cause of the collapse was unknown, but most likely — given the blackout and the aftershock that had awakened most of the street — some kind of explosion in the power supply lines had opened the pit that the building was now sunken into. It had happened late in the night, no one was hurt. His eyes wandered as he spoke, as if he were keeping a look out for something behind me. Behind his head hung a thick swarm of insects, colouring the sky black above the wreckage. I called my contact at the bank and was sent straight to voicemail, walked to the nearest café and took a seat at the high table facing the window. I was eating a bowl of chilli when the door opened and cold air hit the left side of my face. A person came over and sat next to me. I looked up from my chili at his reflection in the windowpane: young man, mid-twenties, short dark hair parted to one side, tall forehead, round rimless glasses. I could see the street through him, but then again his skin was also pale in an airy way. 'Hey, you,' he said, and ordered what I was having. The smell of café burger filled the room when the kitchen door opened, and turned into sweat on the back of my neck. 'Where are you from?' the guy suddenly asked. 'Um... here, actually,' I said, looking down at myself, 'but I've been living abroad for a while now. What gave me away?' 'Your clothes, your suitcase, your glasses,' he said. 'Everything, just your appearance, really. You're not from here.' 'Have I seen you somewhere before?' I said, and regretted it immediately, tried to explain that I didn't mean him but his reflection in the glass, the way I was both seeing and seeing through him. He smelled like eucalyptus and some other kind of aromatic. A big group left the café, and then it was empty like the plane had been empty when I was awakened by the flight attendant, except that now the waiter was gone too and it was quiet in the kitchen. 'I'm going for a cigarette,' the guy said, getting up. 'Do you have an extra?' I asked, even though I didn't smoke. He grabbed his coat from the rack and said yeah and I realised that he probably just wanted some air — so damn quiet in that café — and that he probably preferred to go alone. 'Nice with some smoke out here in the cold,' I said. He nodded and looked at me, his face blue-white in the frozen sun. I looked at our legs in the window and took out my phone to search for a place to stay. I was supposed to be staying in the bank's guest apartment, that is, in one of the rooms that now lay in pieces, spread among other rooms. 'Where are you sleeping tonight?' he asked. I was going to say 'at a friend's,' but that could get awkward if he asked me the address, and I couldn't remember the name of a single hotel. 'I'm not sure yet.' 'You can crash with me. Everything is booked because of that summit meeting.' Neutral gaze, his blank eyes like metal bolts in the cold air. I looked at my phone. 'You don't need to check. I'm telling you the truth.' He lived in an attic studio off Bredgade. The room had no moulding or stucco, its lines as sharp as the lines of his face when the light was dimmed. It shone from a floor lamp pointed upward, so that the ceiling was covered by a disc sun with two eyes in the middle from the filaments. There was a shower cubicle, a steel sink, a refrigerator and a hot plate, a double bed, two chairs and a trestle desk. The window was small, the cracks around it filled with sealant a shade whiter than the yellowish walls. The narrow sides of the room were bare of furniture, but one of the walls was blanketed by a spangled sheet of packaging; empty sweets and crisp packets, cereal boxes, paper and plastic wrappers from lollipops, chewing gum, snack sausages and soda bottles, all from brands unfamiliar to me, as if they had been collected in a parallel universe, where every product was slightly different from the corresponding one in our world, so that you could recognise something as, for example, a chocolate bar, but at the same time find that word an inadequate denomination of it, because you were encountering the object for the very first time, and it was glowing, the wall was glowing with colours I had never seen before. 'Souvenirs,' said Alvin, because that was his name, and threw his coat on the back of a chair. I did the same. Alvin sat down on the bed and pulled off his shoes, and I did the same. 'Nice and warm in here,' he said as he removed his socks — sweet heavy smell of winter feet — and laid them on the radiator. The room was about two hundred square feet, and so sparsely furnished that you couldn't help but register every movement. I looked up and noticed a small, metallic bottle with white waves down its body and a soft plastic straw, sewn into the fabric that held all the wrappers together in a mottled thicket against the wall. This dull and characterless object, whose purpose was to contain and be emptied of a liquid called *POCARI SWEAT*, shone before my eyes with a brilliance that was wildly enticing. I blinked and felt suddenly exhausted, like after a long illness. 'I think I'll take a nap — if that's okay with you?' 'Make yourself at home,' Alvin said. I awoke from a nightmare in which I was being slapped by a floating hand — the rest of the body above the elbow disappeared into white fog — to the sound of Alvin in the shower. The curtain clung to his scrawny legs, itty-bitty, bulging chicken legs. As long as he's not expecting anything in return, I thought to myself, before realising that he was doing just as he would if I weren't there. It had a calming effect on me, like someone sprawled on a bed saying 'I'm not afraid of you,' and so I didn't need to be afraid of him either. It smelled like eucalyptus. Alvin was quiet, only audible in the sound of water hitting his body and falling to the floor in splashes. Trying to be polite, I rolled onto my other side and was playing possum when he stepped out of the shower, and I waited another ten minutes before yawning and saying, 'Nice with a little nap.' 'Take a shower. If you want,' he said, and I did. Afterward, Alvin smoking at the desk with his back to me, I got dressed with the intention of taking a walk, but then realised it was three o'clock in the morning. Still no word from the bank. Alvin offered me a cigarette. I sat on the chair next to him and smoked. The program running on his computer resembled the internal operating system that I was here to help the bank install. When a company of that size purchased that kind of software, they also had to pay for someone to implement it, in which capacity I was to travel from Málaga to Copenhagen six times, this being the fourth. In fact, I appreciated travelling for work, even though it filled me with a sense of randomness, a suspicion that the buildings and the people and the vehicles around me could just as easily be some other ones. It was so random that I had gone to Málaga, and that there was, in Málaga, a company that specialised in the development of operating systems that many companies in the Scandinavian finance sector found to be sublimely compatible with their internal organisational structures, such that I, who spoke Danish and could also get by in Swedish and Norwegian, was hired as a software consultant, despite the fact that I lacked any actual experience in the field. It was as if the contingency of all the circumstances that sent me to Copenhagen or Bergen or Uppsala so thoroughly saturated my experience of those cities that it felt like I wasn't really there. Sometimes my entire working life felt like one big coincidence, or like the inevitability of a network of connections that belonged not to me but to the market, the market of Internal Operating Systems. Alvin clicked between tabs listing various amounts, some of them substantial, some staggering, connected to ID numbers that referred to other numbers, and the screen glowed silver on his forehead. 'Stocks,' I said. 'Is that how you make a living? Actually, I install operating systems for investment banking firms sometimes, but I could never imagine myself...' 'Derivatives,' Alvin said. 'I don't speculate about the future, I trade it.' 'Bonds?' I asked. 'Well, let's start with the farmer,' he sighed, and told me about derivatives, those mechanisms which I now accept as a precondition for the economy, but which at that point made my brain press against my skull and my nose bleed. *The farmer* — who made an agreement with a buyer to sell his next harvest at a predetermined price at a specified date in the future — was the original example of a derivative trader. By doing so, he was able to insure himself against market fluctuations and unpredictable weather. Conversely, the buyer could earn a profit if the value of the crops exceeded the predetermined price. Prior to 1970, derivative trading was largely illegal, seen as a kind of gambling, but by this point, in the year I met Alvin, derivative capital grossly exceeded the capital that came from the production and sale of goods and services, including stocks. For derivatives no longer referred only to the future value of a sack of flour or a ton of rice, but to anything: the price indexes of raw materials, interest rate differentials, exchange rates, credit scores of entire corporations and nations, obviously all in the future. And they were cross-linked and interwoven and resold in large bundles, 'future on future,' Alvin said, handing me a paper towel. 'Forget about the forces of the free market, my friend. Commodity prices no longer refer to any value, past or present — they're just ghosts from the future.' In the morning, when the window was fogged up and Alvin had fallen asleep with the computer on his stomach, I knew that he had told the truth.

After half an hour, we had switched places, so that I could do the clicking while he told me what to click on. I don't know whether it was the friction of the mouse, its smooth, slightly greasy surface, or the amounts being transferred, disappearing and reappearing, inseparable from their ID numbers and in time with my clicking — or the fact that we were actually having a nice time together; Alvin heated up a can of curry soup and bought more cigarettes, and at some point we laughed a lot because I had accidentally bought the right to buy a massive batch of chickens, millions of them, from a farm in Jerusalem a few months from now — in any case, I felt at home in derivative trading, as if it had been waiting for me, and I for it. We brought the computer into bed with us and continued trading on Alvin's stomach. He told me — in a neutral voice and with his eyes on the screen, as he said everything else — that his parents were dead, but that he had inherited some money, which he had grown large enough in stocks to enter the world of derivative trading, where you never actually buy the asset in question but always resell the agreement before the closing date. He mumbled something about a guardian and about 'trading without attachments' and fell asleep. I lay beside him in the pale light of the day outside, joyful and tense, like when my mother was on maternity leave with my little brother and let me watch him while she took her morning shower. Propped up on one elbow, my face a few inches from his, I held my breath to listen to his, afraid it would stop if I was inattentive for a second, and overjoyed every time it repeated. I had arranged his stuffed animals paw-to-paw in a circle around us, so they would be ready for him if he were to wake up. I couldn't sleep, but that was okay, I didn't mind lying in bed, watching Alvin's face twitch, the contours of a dream quivering under his eyelids. Thin skin covered his eyeballs in a way that laid them bare, which made me think that maybe we all sleep with a distant awareness of being watched. At one point, he rolled over and swung his leg over my crotch, and I got a completely unexpected erection. I swear I wasn't sexually aroused or having any fantasies about Alvin — he was beautiful only in a cold, statuesque way — my penis rose merely as a kind of reflex, irrespective of what was behind the contact or could be linked to it. We woke up after noon and went out to get something to eat. On the way, we smoked a cigarette, and the feeling of rust returned to my throat like a memory. The cars on Store Kongensgade idled in traffic, their exhaust calm and white, the faces of cyclists frozen. Roadworks were under way as usual, and Alvin disappeared for a few seconds in the steam rising from the manholes. At the café, he ordered five Secretary's Brunch platters with orange juice and asked to have them brought out together. For ten minutes, he considered each plate one by one as if he were trying to uncover all the sides of the meat and cheese, yogurt and eggs. There was an attentiveness in his gaze that could turn to scepticism, even resentment. Every two minutes, he decisively pushed away another of the brunch platters until he was finally left with one, which he ate without deigning to look at the others. 'You better get used to it,' he said, and explained that it was the only way he could get full. It wasn't so much a matter of being able to choose, or of throwing something away; the idea of surplus didn't interest him.

But the thought that there were a hundred brunch platters just like his was unbearable, which was why he ordered five, always five of everything. That way he could pretend to limit the offering in order to reject the four least real, 'to isolate the actual brunch from the imitations,' he said. I thought it was ridiculous. Alvin took out his phone and showed me pictures of him at various shiny plastic tables, with fast-food meals in front of him. He was sickly pale in the way that people tend to be in pictures from the nineties. 'This is me at KFC when the first one opened in Denmark... Me at the first Burger King, did you know they proposed a Whopper—Big Mac mash-up, in the name of world peace?... Here I am at Subway... Domino's... The Bagel Company when they opened their first shop on Gothersgade in '94. I swear, tasting these things for the first time was completely... how should I say, unique. Like I was tasting exactly them and only them. I always take pictures the first time.' The pictures had clearly been taken by someone else. It made me weirdly sad to imagine Alvin walking up to the counter and asking to have his picture taken, and the employee, out of politeness and because there weren't any other customers at that time of day, following him to his table to do so. Alvin looked so alone and happy in all the pictures. When we went up to the counter to pay, my card was declined, the one I usually used when I travelled to Denmark for work or to visit my younger brother. I often wondered whether my ex-wife still lived here, how it would feel to run into her again now that my jealousy, which had entirely blocked my longing for her the first few months in Málaga, had disappeared. That was the worst thing about her infidelity: how the anger and powerlessness and all the other jilted feelings ended up dissolving my memory of her into a cloud of pornographic images, and when they finally left me, it was as if she had died. While Alvin took care of the bill, I turned around, ran to our table and shovelled some eggs and pastrami from one of his scrapped brunch platters into my mouth. Back in his room, he asked if I wanted to borrow some money to cover my expenses now that my bank account was sunk in the ground. I said no, it was more than enough that he was letting me spend the night. 'It's not a handout,' he said. 'I think we can help each other. I'm planning to look at some silver tonight.' Two hours later, I had used the monstrous sum he had transferred into my Spanish bank account to purchase stocks in silver mines. Shortly after, he signed an agreement to buy a quantity of silver so large that my shares rose almost 30 percent over the course of the following day. This inspired a number of other people to invest in silver, which in turn increased the value of Alvin's derivative, and by the time he resold it two days later, we had both earned a month's salary, or at least what that would have been for me. During the intervening night, we had started the same process with another asset and its derivative, and so we continued for the rest of the week, each process morphing into the next and the nights merging in cigarette smoke and the light from our computer screens. There was something tender about the way he grabbed his screen with both hands, looking it in the eye, whenever a crucial deal was about to be signed, and then when it was: no celebration, only an affirmative nod. Even his slightest movements affected me, the way he moved in harmony with the room's inventory or as an extension of it: his right foot jiggling on the leg of the desk chair, right hand resting on the mouse, forearm parallel with the edge of the table and opposite wall; the gentle, pious way he paced across the room, like when you're carrying a bowl full of soup, which he often was, bringing it to me and sitting down to tell me more about derivative trading. He wanted me to understand that it was an 'effective art of promise and expectation.' 'You need to learn to think of the commodity as existing in advance,' he said, 'like when there's something you're looking forward to. As soon as the idea of a given product is on the market, it *acts*, and a sewer is constructed, a sewer that drains from the future in which the product will be sold, back in time, back to us. A sewer that you can of course only move through in one direction, against the current so to speak, but where you can also stop at every stride and sell your spot for a profit or at a loss, depending on how bright the light at the end of the tunnel is shining in our collective eyes at exactly that point in time, yeah, sorry for the death image, it doesn't have to do with death at all, because you can, as I was saying, usually crawl out before you get to the end, through one of the more or less rusty and financially attractive hatches in the wall, or switch places with another sewer-walker, you know, make a *swap*, right, and the light was never really death, but the commodity, which has a life too, it can be sold too, don't forget that.' It felt like we were lying in a tent on top of a tall and sad building. Nights flew by. 'Alvin,' I might say in a cautious voice when it had been quiet for many minutes, feeling it was okay to speak to him in that way, 'hey, Alvin?' 'Yeah?' 'Are you asleep?' 'If I was, I wouldn't be answering you, would I?' 'No... but Alvin, you were on fire today! You demolished that municipality when you sold them that swap loan. As soon as the interest rates start to rise, and the trigger is released...' 'My friend,' he said, 'of course the money we're making is money other people are losing. That's just the nature of derivatives. But that doesn't mean that we're doing it *because* we want others to lose.' 'But that kind of leverage is completely integrated...' 'Yes, exactly, that's what makes it possible for the market to even exist. It's so obvious that it doesn't make any sense to think about it.' I couldn't do it myself, but I could easily imagine that it would be possible for someone with many years in the business to refrain from rejoicing in those who were necessarily losing. To edit them out of the image, by an act of will working slowly and covertly inside you, so that in the end only your own victory remains, and you've completely forgotten that you've done it, that you've edited them out. Where does that ability come from? How can you give it up? When the window was wet with condensation, the day flooding white through it, and Alvin had fallen asleep, I carefully closed his computer and put it on the floor. The sound of the CPU fan ceased like someone had stopped breathing. Alvin's face was hard and strikingly white against his dark hair. His lips pressed together in a line that slanted a little into his mouth. I was overcome by sadness, a big, grey-white feeling, and at its edge hovered a dark object that I couldn't grasp. Occasionally, I glimpsed a corner or a fracture, but as soon as I tried to uncover more of it, it disappeared, and then when I wanted to return to my flimsy starting point, that was gone too. I wanted to cry. I missed my ex-wife and the few friends I used to have here, all the ones who let me down or whom I abandoned as soon as they showed they needed me. Suddenly, I felt like I had given up my life back then, ceded control to someone else. My life was lonely and irrelevant. Alvin's hands weren't quite folded, but intertwined in a forced grasp, as if they had been trying to find each other when sleep came over him. 'I've never been to Romania.' I gave a start under the duvet. 'Have you ever been to Romania?' I heard as Alvin's lips moved again. 'No,' I whispered. 'Never.' We arrived in Bucharest late at night and took a cab from the airport to the hotel. Still slightly drunk from the flight, we threw ourselves on the Bordeaux-red bedspread, wrecking the two towel swans. It felt like we were inaugurating the room, just lying there with our computers on our bellies, checking stock prices and receiving offers on their derivatives, and an hour later — when eucalyptus streamed from Alvin's shower and intermingled with the smell of our socks on the radiator — I felt at home, and had entirely forgotten that we were in Romania. 'Your turn!' Alvin shouted. I threw off my clothes, squeezed past him at the sink and stepped into the bathtub. 'Why didn't you use the free shampoo?' I asked through the shower curtain. 'Someone else can use it,' he said, handing me a little torso-shaped bottle. 'I discovered this in South Africa in '08 and it's the only thing I've used since. Give it a try.' I squeezed a little blob out of the bottle — *aromatherapy: stress relief* — and massaged it into my scalp. A prickly coolness penetrated and settled under my skull like an internal shower cap made of a hundred tiny massaging hands. 'Fantastic,' I said, feeling the steam relax my airways as I rinsed out the shampoo. 'Yeah, right?' said Alvin. 'And hey, didn't you say something about your back hurting? It's also great for knots and tension.' Unable to reach the painful spot under my shoulder blade, I must have groaned, because Alvin said 'Let me,' and stuck his hands through the opening in the shower curtain. 'Don't worry, I'll stay out here. Give me some shampoo.' I squeezed a blob into his hand, olive green and viscous, and turned my back to him. He moved up from my lower back until I said 'Oooooeeee, yes, yes, right there!' and then he pressed until the knot loosened and dissolved into my body. 'You seem very tense in general.' He continued up my neck and down along the left side of my spine. 'These essential oils come from a species of eucalyptus called fever tree. Isn't that a wonderful name, fever tree? It's because people used to plant tons of them in areas with malaria. They dry out the swamps where the mosquito larvae hatch.' He was now squatting on the other side of the curtain, massaging the back of my thighs. 'The active ingredient in the oil, eucalyptol, is pretty strong. Sometimes, when it's very hot and there's no wind in the forest, eucalyptus trees emit so much volatile oil that even a little spark, from a cigarette for example, can trigger an explosion and start a fire. Turn around.' A slap on my calf, I turned my chest toward him. There was so much steam in the room that I could no longer see the opening in the shower curtain or what was on the other side. I leaned my head back and watched the water fall out of the air like warm rain made especially for me. 'More shampoo.' I squeezed a blob into his bowl-shaped hands. They distributed the liquid between themselves and began to massage me from the forehead down.

Alvin kept talking, but I was no longer listening to what he was saying. The words splashed out of the air like blobs of sound with the water, running down my face and chest with his hands, his finger pads pressing against my muscles so I could feel their soreness. The camphoric cold heat spread with his hands. From my groin they moved in arcs around my genitals and continued down my thighs. Eucalyptus, like a living suit under my skin, covered my entire body, apart from the places his hands had left untouched: my eyes, mouth, groin and ass. And because of the intense sensation all around them, my eyes, mouth, groin and ass disappeared, or they felt like lumps of nothingness, like infinite holes that would swallow anything that came near. I registered a tightening sensation at the base of my stomach, growing in intensity, like dark matter contracting into itself, and as his hands stretched to reach around my ankles, and his cheek came into view against the curtain, the sensation became so small it disappeared. For maybe ten seconds, I was in a funnel of time, seeing only myself at the other end. It was very lonely. Afterward, we lay in bed with towels wrapped around our waists and shared a cigarette. The next day we rode tirelessly around Bucharest on the kick scooters that Alvin had brought in his duffel bag. The pavements were smooth and nicely droning to roll across. Ornamented buildings in harmonically round shapes were interspersed with massive tower blocks from the Communist era. A man was standing in front of the entrance to the metro with out-stretched arms, his hands full of cucumber peelers. From a string tied around his neck, long, dark green peels dangled, sweating in the sun, as evidence of the efficacy of his product. Another man handed me a sheet of paper with a strange illustration on a background of twilight beach lagoon: a Barbie-like figure in a white bikini straddling a rocket headed toward the upper right corner, the rocket transparent, so you could see its three layers: three penises contained within each other, gradually increasing in length and thickness along the measuring tape running parallel to them. I folded the piece of paper and put it in the pocket of my khakis. A woman, her eyes pure iris, dropped a watermelon at a pedestrian crossing. Impossible to see the sky behind power lines stretched between telephone poles. *CABINET PSIHOLOGIC* was written on a yellowish house with cracks in the walls. A group of kids observed a beetle trapped inside a glass vase turned upside down on the asphalt. Water like dust fell onto my boiled skin from valves in the café awnings. Cash made of plastic in Alvin's cold hands, impossible to rip, soak, set on fire. He said, 'What's mine is yours.' 'Thanks' died unsaid on my lips, as if someone had placed a long, cold finger over them. I remember all the things he used to do: pelvis against the handlebars of the scooter, centre of gravity sinking into his knees, he leans into the bumps on the road. The slight irony in the way his fingers hold a cigarette. That day, even the planes were beautiful. Broken air. Plants shooting up through broken asphalt. Rancid smell of beef and other dead animals in a market on the city outskirts. A gorgeous butcher shop, wasps floating in blood. 'I never use public transport,' Alvin said. We were eating breakfast in dark-green patio chairs in the fenced car park of a petrol station. We had taken a busy road lined with tower blocks and car repair shops, a good hour past the railway tracks that bordered the city to the west. Under umbrellas five yards from us, a group of men in work clothes were drinking beer and smoking, with their eyes on the TV. You couldn't hear anything over the traffic, but the outdated television set and their silence were enough to make me feel like I was sitting in a bar or community centre with its own slow kind of time. Most of them were about my age, one closer to Alvin's. The skin of their faces was hard and dry like the skin of hands. Their heads followed the waitress, who I think was the owner's daughter, not more than twenty years old. Every ten minutes, she would come out with a new beverage and chocolate bar for Alvin and me, since Alvin had ordered a large assortment and paid extra to have her serve them to us one by one. Now she was filling our plastic cups with a black liquid that resembled Coke but that turned out to be terribly bitter, almost antiseptic. 'When you travel by scooter, you don't miss a thing,' Alvin said. 'There aren't those breaks in continuity, like when you arrive at one place from another underground or in the cabin of a plane... Oh fuck, I've tried this before! It's just Romanian Chinò!' He held the cup in front of his face, disgusted. 'Exactly this... I've had this before!' he said, and dumped the liquid onto the pavement. He gathered his composure for a moment before continuing: 'But still, it's like the city stays at the level of surface. I think it's because of the speed, how everything just slides by. You can't pretend you're able to see through any of it.' And then my cup was yanked out of my hand and emptied like Alvin's. I looked up at a tall, sunburned man in work clothes. He put my cup back on the table and nodded toward the street. We followed his gaze and looked back at him, perplexed. 'Yes,' he said, looking me in the eye with crossed arms and a didactic expression on his face, patient and determined, and I felt ashamed. 'What does he want?' Alvin asked. 'I think he wants us to leave,' I said. 'But we're in the middle of a tasting here—' 'Yes,' the man repeated. One of the younger men in a black tank top came out of the shop with the rest of our purchases in a bag, which he dropped into Alvin's lap. 'Okay,' Alvin said, gathering the empty wrappers and cans. We got up, unfolded our scooters and rolled away, bottles and papers hanging out of Alvin's pockets, bulging out of his duffel bag, clinging to him. Back in the city centre, we passed an exact replica of the Arc de Triomphe. The boulevard was forty yards wide, divided by a bed of flowers and a fountain lit up in neon colours: blue, pink, silver. There were clothing stores with names like Fashion Victim and Shopping Is Cheaper Than Therapy. In the old city centre, we stopped at a street theatre, folded up our scooters and stood among the other spectators. I could feel the body heat, not only from the people standing closest to me, but like a homogeneous cloud that everyone in the audience was simultaneously producing and contained within. Everyone's attention was focused on the stage. The sun had set but its light was still in the sky, a pale blue afterglow cancelling out the dark for a little longer. Some had children on their shoulders, others leaned their heads back and laughed into the sky whenever something funny happened. On stage about twenty yards in front of us were two people on stilts, one with a snare drum and the other with some sort of little horn hanging from her neck, playing a medieval tune mixed with a bit of jazz.

At their feet, two petite figures, costumed as knights in red and green, approached each other and exchanged what sounded like hostilities. I repeated their words out loud. A peculiar combination of sounds I didn't understand entered my body and came out of my mouth; I didn't know the language, but it made me high. Just as involuntarily, I repeated the next thing that was said, and Alvin responded by repeating the lines of the other knight. Now they were throwing themselves forward, tightly interlocked at the elbows, using all their weight to drag each other to the ground. The one in green gave in and took a step backward to keep his footing, tipping his upper body back so that the one in red was lifted into the air, where he hovered horizontally for a few seconds before he landed, sending the one in green into the air in turn. Their struggle turned into a dance, their bodies like leaves somersaulting in the wind without letting go of each other. They kept shouting, the dance an extension of their struggle, and we kept repeating what they said. Abruptly, the knights came to a stop in the grip with which the dance had started. Their feet yielded beneath them and their bodies lay outstretched, almost horizontal in the air. And then they fell to the ground with their foreheads pressed against each other. It was quiet. They raised their faces and looked each other in the eye. One of them said something, loud and clear, but with a tenderness too, and as I repeated what he said, applause erupted around us. I turned to Alvin and repeated the line, yelling as loudly as I could, again and again, until I felt a poke on my shoulder. A young woman, laughing, said in English, 'Do you know what you just said to your son?' 'No,' I said, 'he's just my friend.' 'Your Romanian is terrible.' 'But what did I say? What did it mean?' 'You said, "My brother, you may never leave me again."' I don't know whether Alvin heard her, he looked as indifferent as usual: horizontal mouth and metal-bolt eyes, not a single direction in that face. Back at the hotel, we showered one at a time. 'Use my shampoo,' he said, squeezing past me. I can't describe the joy I felt lying next to him, all of my muscles exhausted, unable to fall asleep. The darkness was thick, our breathing heavy, but each of us knew the other wasn't asleep. Our awareness filled the room like something large and encompassing, and if I was inside it, then Alvin was too. Later that night, I heard him sit up, swing his legs over the edge of the bed and put on his clothes. He got up and gently lifted the duffel bag that had been packed in advance, but couldn't avoid a little clinking from the bottles and paused for a second. He stood still, probably trying to hear whether he had woken me up, though I prefer to think of those seconds as seconds of doubt. That way he can stay, as strong and indefinable as ever, sleeping, trading, showering in my memory. After he closed the door behind him, I lay in bed for several hours without turning on the light. When morning streamed white into the room, I packed my things and left the hotel on the scooter he had left behind. At the airport they told me that I didn't have any money. None of my bank accounts existed anymore, my debit cards were untethered, their ties fluttered in the wind. I laid all the cash I had on the counter and was told that I probably had enough for a train ticket. The continuousness of the trip calmed me down. Back in Copenhagen, I went to the bank hoping to get in touch with one of the employees who knew me and could probably help me. The ruins were still there. I climbed a piece of marble at the edge and looked over the wreckage, which lay spread across a large expanse, torn up like a lake full of rubbish, steel grey and grey-white, yellowish with wood here and there. Above hung a dense swarm of insects and a dark, sweet smell like rotting tea leaves. I broke into a run across the wreckage, calculating my leaps and landing deftly, all at once feeling young and in control of my body. I found a pit between two big pieces of marble that was fairly accessible and appeared to flatten out a few yards below. Holding on to the marble, I lowered myself down, finding a foothold in the jagged walls. The air became heavy, the insect sky framed by the opening of the pit; my toes grazed the ground, which seemed solid. I let myself fall, hunched over and continued on all fours through the narrow tunnel that opened darkly in front of me. The marble was hard against my knees; in places, I had to pull them up to my belly or arch my back to avoid sharp edges and protrusions. The tunnel narrowed and turned, and I followed its path on my elbows, dragging my torso behind me, until suddenly my head was poking into something that resembled a room — a big hole created when the building had collapsed: steel, plaster and wood held up by large rock fragments. But the materials were all so irregular, haphazardly placed and full of cracks leading to other tunnels, that it was impossible to get a sense of the room's dimensions. Bank employees lay curled up, in broken and cocooned positions dictated by the uneven walls of the pit, with computers in their laps or on their stomachs. Their faces were dirty and pale, some were wearing masks in the dusty air. 'Are you looking for someone?' a young man asked, and came over to help me out of the wall. 'No,' I said, and managed to stutter the name of the system administrator. 'Follow me,' he said, and showed me through the cracks and holes, crawling, climbing and snaking ahead depending on the spatial parameters. Something about the writhing way he moved his body gave me the sense that he was being pulled or sucked through the passageways. That some subterranean intelligence or will had laid the bank in ruins and was now forcing its employees into new shapes. People had set up workspaces in the most unexpected places. Cables drew electricity in every direction, illuminating the connections between them. I imagined a monstrous and hollowed-out architecture, the crushed building materials poured into a colossal anthill, held together by internet waves and the fermented, organic breath that swelled in every tunnel. A choir of fingers on keyboards rose from the depths. We slid around a warped steel plate, legs first, and into another room. At its centre, the system administrator was seated on a pillow in lotus pose with three screens in front of her. A mouse rested on a hunk of marble by her right hand. 'What the hell,' she said, and looked up at me, laughing. 'Weren't you supposed to be here ten days ago?' 'Yes,' I said, and started to make up an excuse that made no sense to me, and took a step forward, kicking some small rocks with my foot. After maybe ten seconds, they hit the water. 'Don't worry about it,' she said, dismissing my apology with a wave of her hand. 'Let's get to it, then.'

Bad Mexican Dog

There's something special about the beach because I'm a beach boy. Something's supposed to happen down at the beach. I remember the beach in Essaouira, Marseille, San Juan, where it didn't happen, and every night I looked up at a sky so blue between power lines it made my face hurt. Not because there's anything special about the sky, only that it's sometimes a very hard blanket stretched tight over my head, making me feel an impassable distance. If I was in heaven I'd be looking up at Earth, blue between power lines. I'm a fifteen-year-old thin and brown-haired boy with green eyes. I move with a little curve in my back like a panther, small and bashful because no one notices me. Now I'm in Cancún, Mexico, and I've been standing in front of the counter for a while without being seen. It's early in the morning, and the owner is fighting with his wife about a boy who quit without notice just today.

I picked this beach club because the lion on its flag reminded me of an English tourist with a full beard who gave a big tip in Essaouira, Marseille, San Juan. The owner turns to look at me with short-fuse eyes, but before he gets the chance to tell me off I say this:

'Word is you need a boy?'

'We always need boys,' the owner replies, 'but are you a real beach boy?'

I say yes, I'm made of the right stuff, and list my previous employments.

'All right then, follow me,' he says, and walks around to the back of the square bamboo hut, which is also the club's bar and reception. He opens the door to an elongated storage room. Towels, fans, sunscreen, after-sun. Half-litre bottles of mineral water *naturelle* in a cooler. The morning sun makes spots on my skin through the bamboo wall. The owner throws a pair of black swim trunks and a white undershirt on the bench and tells me to get changed. Then he leaves the room, and while I undress, I can see, past the bar through a chink in the wall, the sky and the ocean so blue between beach chairs it tickles my crotch. There's something I'm here for, there's something I have to do. In the sand in front of the bench, an elongated pool has been dug and covered with pool-blue plastic. The water is full of small jellyfishy blobs swimming around like living water. My legs are too short to reach, but I can feel the slimy dampness under the soles of my feet.

'You know the deal?' shouts the owner, and opens the door as I'm pulling the swim trunks over my hips. 'You keep your tips. The rest is mine.'

I agree, and he straps a fanny pack over my swim trunks. There's a pouch for lotions on one side, and four round pockets that'll stretch for water bottles. I can feel the owner's chest hair against my shoulder as he suits me up. He says the other boys will tell me everything I need to know about life on the beach.

There are 480 beach chairs in total, 24 rows of 20, and we're 6 boys, that's 4 rows or 80 chairs for each. If you've got your own section under control, if none of your guests need anything — beverages, lotioning up, a little shade or face fanning — then you can try your luck up by the entrance. It's on those twenty metres of boardwalk that stretch from the reception desk down to the beach chairs that you have to make the right impression. This is where I get to see the other boys in action, get to know their style. This is where I see Immanuel.

When the French lady in the sun hat is halfway down the boardwalk, he lifts one foot and takes aim with a decisive gait. But he does it cool, and the way he makes his hips tilt as he walks, long waves of bone and tawny brown skin pulling him across the sand, makes it happen in slow motion in front of me: each step reveals all of its stages, from the heel strike to the sole worming toward the pads of his toes, and the sand jumps little angel hops around his heel. My eyes slide up to his hips again, and I can see his pelvis tilting with each step from side to side, and I think of crustaceans and mottled fish swimming around in the shell of his pelvis, in the light blue ocean lapping against his pubic bone. It's very powerful, Immanuel's groin, rocking up the boardwalk as everything else about him fades, his long black hair and tawny brown skin, and when he's ten feet away from the lady in the sun hat something ashen has come over him, like an old waiter at a French café.

'Welcome to the beach club, madam. What if I were your personal boy for the duration of your stay? Shade, sun, sunscreen, massage and cold drinks, whatever you need?'

And the lady with the sun hat says thanks for the offer and hands her bag to Immanuel, and he winks at me as they walk by. He'll make good money on her, sure as the ocean is blue.

Then it's my turn, I strut straight ahead with a little feline curve in my back toward the English couple on the boardwalk so they can't not see me, but they don't see me until we're a few feet away from each other and I say, 'Good morning, what if I were your personal boy—' but by then I've already missed my chance to make a natural break in their path and offer myself, so they know they want me without knowing I want them — I didn't hit the beat like Immanuel — and the man waves his hand disapprovingly.

Getting yourself a side gig and some extra cash: you get one shot a day. So I trot restlessly up and down through my 4 rows of 20 and offer to lotion them up and fan their faces. I change their towels and adjust the parasols to follow the path of the sun in the sky, getting bored at the zenith. In the afternoon, the guests start to fry, and I rub sunscreen and after-sun all over their bodies. As I'm straddling a Swedish man lying on his belly with two belts of flesh over his loins, I see Ginger, the English boy, giving it a go up on the boardwalk. He's whiter than the sand, though the sand is white as the coconut filling in a Bounty bar, and his hair shines copper in the sun.

He's beautiful, Ginger, but his gait is a bit too bovine, very thin knees, he doesn't exude that supple, light-on-the-toes feeling you look for in a boy at all. A beach boy can't look like he's obeying gravity too much, I think. The Swede's flesh belts slip between my fingers. As I'm holding them tight and pulling them apart so I can rub the sunscreen deep into his back, I see Jia, the Chinese boy, heading toward two German women, waddling carelessly, like his bones and joints aren't fully formed. With his bulging round belly and small hips, he's a real boy, maybe the most boyish of us all. The Germans take the bait right away. One of my hands has disappeared between the flesh belts closing around my wrist. I rearrange the organs in there, pull out a kidney and fling it across the sky, and see myself trailing behind it like a shooting star or just a seagull maybe, but I'm a beach boy. That's the contract I signed.

Then it's nighttime, and I'm sitting on the bench in the changing room next to Immanuel. His skin is hard and smooth like stained wood. He peels an orange and slices into the flesh with his knife, and orange fills the room. The sun is in front of me now because the sun sets in the ocean. He feeds me the sliced-off flesh, raises the hunks to my mouth on the blade of the knife: a hard metallic flavour beneath the fresh sweetness. In his other hand, he's holding the sliced wedges together in a bouquet, the long white string lying flaccid in the centre, held together at the bottom by a little circle of peel. He loosens the wedges and spreads them into glistening tentacles, a coral, he says, and pulls the white string erect. 'See, that's the dick,' he says, laughing, and I laugh too, and he shoves the whole thing into his mouth, juice dripping down his chin. Afterward we're silent, and Immanuel takes my dick in his hand. I rest my arm on top of his arm and do the same to him, up and down. Through the chink in the wall, the sun makes a window of light on his stomach. I can see the ocean in it. It's throbbing in my hand. Squirt of thick white juice, first Immanuel and then me, turns orange in the sun lands in the pool-blue pool under our feet, as if the horizon is emanating from our groin, and for a second I remember a room behind the ocean. There are things I have to do, things I have to get done while I'm here.

'Immanuel?' I ask.

'What's up?' he says. 'And hey, just call me Manuel, it's so much with that first syllable.'

'Manuel, how do you do what you do up on the boardwalk?'

'I take a guess. I guess where they're from and how much money they have and then I try to imitate the waiters they know from back home. But you have to make yourself completely blank on the inside. If you want to look like their idea, you have to become the thing.'

'Does that always work for you?'

'If they're old anyway, then they like the comfort of it. But if they're in their twenties or thirties, they'd rather not know you're doing it for their sake, they don't want you speaking English to them in their own accent and all that crap. So whenever I see them with, for example, SKINNY MEXICAN BOY in their eyes, I say LET ME AUTHENTICATE THAT FOR YOU, but I say it inside and just do it.'

So, the next morning I'm standing there looking at the beach with its 480 beach chairs, 24 rows of 20. The rows look like giant tapeworms, each chair its own segment, or they're running through the sand like rivers of meltwater trickling into the ocean. They're the ribs of the coast. Then I get what Manuel meant, and I say it to myself up by the entrance when the German woman comes walking backlit down the boardwalk. I make myself blank and let her eyes wander over my front, which gets very hot while the wind cools my back, and when I greet her, it's with a fresh Mexican accent on my tongue, and she says yes, certainly I can be her personal boy.

During the next five hours, I lotion her up and fetch her cold drinks from the bar. When she gets too hot, she raises her hand and points at her face: I get down on my knees and fan it. Then she tells me to get lost and come back in ten, and as I'm walking away I can feel the cold in my back, as if that side of me has withdrawn, turned away from her and the sun. I jog up and down my 4 rows of 20 and tend to the other guests while I can. Fortunately, Jia and Ginger are helping out with my section. Manuel is taking care of the French lady with the sun hat. Today she asked specifically for him. At the zenith we're all really busy, everyone wants water and light breezes and sunscreen for their bodies. Ginger stumbles in the sand with both hands full and lands on a young woman, his face between her butt cheeks. She screams and her boyfriend jumps up and grabs Ginger by the neck. He's gotten up and is saying sorry with his hands above his head. I start running toward them, screaming that it was an accident, but the boyfriend doesn't hear me; he only sees PERVERTED ASSHOLE STICKING HIS NOSE BETWEEN

MY GIRLFRIEND'S LEGS. He forgets that Ginger is a boy and boys aren't interested in that kind of thing. Ginger falls onto his side with blood coming out of his mouth; long red squirt turns orange in the sun lands on white sand. The boyfriend straddles him and lets loose on his face. In his rage, he grabs a rock, thick red pool next to Ginger's head. Then he gets up and turns, flees along the water, and she runs after him. Me and Jia hurry to bring Ginger's body up into the changing room before the other guests see the hole in his head.

After the zenith, our work rhythm falls into sync with the sun and my sleepiness. My head is throbbing like the temples of the beach, blood is pumping under the sand. The German woman says goodbye and gives me a nice tip, but by now the cold has crept into my back, which she can't see, and turned into a hole inside me. During the last hours of the afternoon, I stop multiple times to look at the things I think are beautiful: the beach chairs, 480 in 24 rows of 20. The parasols that we move with the chairs to follow the path of the sun in the sky. The other boys wandering up and down along the rows in their sections, offering their services. The ocean topped by waves, and it's like the beauty of all these things goes into my body and turns into a pain that keeps the hole open. I'm thinking: The ocean is beautiful without the power to keep itself blue and postcard-like all the time. It's beautiful without the will to spare the ships sailing on it tonight. A massive pool of complete obedience. The contract it's signed. And at the same time, I know there are sides of the ocean I can't see, there are sides of the beach chairs and parasols that withdraw and turn their backs to me, and there's a hole in every boy.

When me and Manuel have gotten changed, orange in the room and the sun a window to the ocean squirt of thick white juice orange in the pool-blue pool, we carry Ginger's body out to the beach. The sand, the ocean and the sky are the same shade of black. The wind is cold against my face and makes the flagpoles groan, and things we don't know make sounds that mingle with the ocean's. The beach chairs appear as we pass them one by one. The sand laps against our bare legs. I'm holding Ginger's arms, Manuel his ankles, and as we're walking down with the body between us, I get a strange feeling. It's not romantic or tender because it's not concentrated in any one place, like my stomach or my crotch, but spread all through my body. As if in the changing room I put on a nice new dress, an imperceptibly tight dress made of the knowledge that I'm here with Manuel and that I'll be seeing him again tomorrow.

We kneel and lay Ginger's body down in the sand. A little while later, Jia and the other boys join us with six buckets of water from the pool in the changing room. We dig out the shape of a body in the sand where the boyfriend split Ginger's head with the rock, and fill it with the water from the buckets. Hundreds of small white squirts swim around in it like living water. We grab his arms and legs and lower the body into the hole. The water splashes a little before it calms down and covers it fully, a thin layer over his face and stomach. Steam rises in the cool air. In a pentagon around the hole, we plant five parasols upside down in the sand, twist them down into the viscous layers. The last three inches of the shafts sticking out of the sand we grease with after-sun before getting on our knees and letting our assholes slide slowly down around them. We look at Ginger's body as Manuel sings monotonously:

We believe in Ginger / working honestly and patiently / many hours in the hole inside ourselves / Our desire for Ginger breaks loose / from Ginger / and travels through the hole over the greatest / distance / until it no longer belongs to us / We believe in Ginger ...

Manuel repeats the verse, and we join in one by one, rocking on the shafts. We sing while looking at Ginger's body. It lasts for hours. Once in a while, the steam takes on colours, fluorescent blue, red and purple. Now and then a squirt of thick white juice that comes to life in the water. And when the after-sun and our secretions run dry on the shaft, the pain and the blood begin to run. White squirts in the water gather around Ginger's skin and coalesce into a suit of jelly: the lines of his body blur, the body flickers. I can't separate my own voice from the others' assholes from the hole deeper inside me where the pain and foreign blood run down hollow parasol shafts soaking the sandy soil below the basin. A pool of colour whirls at our knees. Then Manuel's voice stands out from the choir, dissonant. The rest of us join in tentatively, one sound at a time, until the words take shape and we sing in unison:

Desire for Ginger comes back through us / Desire for Ginger / as he is: the desire to create him / Ginger / as he is to create him / The two become one ...

The water lights up and changes from blood red to purple to orange teeming with pink dots. A slimy fog in the same colours rises and condenses in the vague outline of a body webbed with veins. A glowing creature is now visible, hovering above the basin. Suddenly it hits me that I'm thinking about dead Ginger, not that he should live again, and in the same second the creature becomes flesh and falls into the basin with a splash.

Later, we walk into one of the early-morning spots with dirty tiles and white light, where the concrete workers and taxi drivers are drinking their coffee. I like the people who work at night. We pour our tips into Jia's hands, and he goes up to buy eggs, toast and orange juice with all the money. The liquid is very cold and pulpy in my throat. In a bowl on the table, there are wrinkly oranges that Manuel cuts into little corals. 'This one is Ginger!' yells Ginger, and mashes one of them with the ashtray, squirt of thin yellow juice turns grey in the electric light lands on the tiles. We laugh and stick our fingers between the tentacles of our corals, pull the long white strings to see who has the longest and laugh again. Afterward, we play a game where we take turns impersonating people from the club.

'Manuel?' I say into the darkness on our way back home.

'What's up?' he says. 'And just call me Manu, it's so much with that last syllable.'

'Manu, how did we do that to Ginger?'

'It was Ginger who decided to come back.'

'But how?'

'I don't know, that's just how it is. Most people want to come back, even though they forget everything they saw while they were gone. That's the contract they signed... Anyway, this is me.'

He lays a hand on the back of my neck and gives it a squeeze before turning down a dusty road with concrete buildings like mine. He says good night and winks, and as he's walking away with his back to me, he shrinks into a little cat and lopes away, and I would like to run after him, then we could be two small cats lying together talking in his bed.

Afterward, I keep walking, looking up at the sky between power lines. It's a very dark blue, and at the same time lit up by a secret little light because the sun isn't here yet, but whispers up over the sloping of the globe that it's on its way. My face hurts a little. A thin memory of something important that's supposed to happen on the beach. A room behind another room. I can't make it home anyway, so I find a bench near the club and sleep for an hour and a half. I dream that night has fallen, but the guests haven't gone home yet. They're still lying there, immobile, with their eyes closed or sunglasses on, as if they haven't realised that the sun has gone down and it's cold now. Then all the big cats get a whiff of the fried skin steaming in the cool night, jump out of the trees on the boulevard along the beach and flay all the guests into little pieces. Streamers of flesh and guts hang over the beach chairs, 24 rows of 20.

I can move with a little curve in my back like a panther, but I rarely do it because I'm a beach boy. I've sort of taken Manu's place, because he's taking care of the French lady with the sun hat, like he's done for the last three weeks. She pays him a fixed salary, and they've started to develop what I think you'd call a personal relationship. He learns ten new French words a day. She asks about his life, also about the time before he started at the club. She's like a pool in your backyard, says Manu, that you can't use anyway, so you might as well throw your trash and old furniture in it. When the guests come walking down the boardwalk from the entrance, I make myself blank and approach them. LET ME AUTHENTICATE THAT FOR YOU, I say if I see them with, say, SKINNY MEXICAN BOY or SCANDINAVIAN SIMPLICITY in their eyes, but I say it inside and just do it. I've gotten good, maybe as good as Manu, and I know that the owner has noticed. He's hired a new boy and pulls me aside one night to ask if I want to make a little extra. Obviously I say yeah. He gives me a bag with a video camera and some official-looking documents. He shows me pictures of a young couple and tells me play-by-play how it's supposed to go down. He's printed it in typewriter font on a piece of paper, which I read over and over in bed before I fall asleep. The next day, when the couple shows up, I make sure I'm their personal boy, and I do exactly like the owner said, and it works, I get it all on tape.

When I get back later that afternoon, there's chaos at the club because Manu is curled up in a foetal position on the French woman's belly, so the new boy has to cover two sections by himself. I jump in right away, and the next hour I rub sunscreen and after-sun onto so much skin that my hands get tired of impressions: smooth, hard skin like stained wood. Elastic, speckled, suntanned skin, falling like curtains around my fingers. Or a gooey, vaguely greasy pelt, but it doesn't mean anything to me. The skins are sticky, the sand is burning, the woman's foot tasted like orange peel. My nerves are shaking and I don't have the energy to respond to them. The other boys disappear behind parasols and suntanned hands hanging in the air and waving me over: I run around and fan faces, give massages, fetch drinks. I'm exhausted. The sun is shining.

As we're sitting on the bench in the changing room, glittering knife orange in orange sun fallen in wedges and the ocean, Manu gets up and pulls me down into the pool. There's a different light, a fluorescent blue fog that makes my skin tight and slimy.

'I'm not mad,' he says, and hugs me from behind.

We spoon, the water covering half my face. Manu holds me, but at the same time pushes against me in a small way, his face between my shoulder blades, his knees against my thighs, so maybe I'm the one holding him. We stay that way for a long time. I can't make out the different parts of his body anymore, his chest, arms, feet, forehead, he's just a little shrimp on my back. The other boys are somewhere in the pool too. We're all very small. I want to cry. I breathe in through my left nostril, which is above the water, and breathe out through the right. I close my left eye and keep the other open, so the surface of the water becomes a lid on the world. The bubbles of oxygen coming out of my nostril look like cats jumping up and down, exploding the second they hit the surface. As if they can only exist at a distance from it. But at least there they're wild and agile, and kind of funny too. Suddenly I get water in my left nostril; the water level has risen, and I cough. I sit up and look at Manu lying there, crying silently.

'Manu,' I say. 'Manu, shouldn't we just go home, together? I'm so tired.'

'You go,' he says without looking at me, an eye on either side of the surface of the water. 'I want to stay here a little longer.'

We were about to leave the club when the boy with the pretty green eyes, who had been bringing us water and snacks and asking if we needed anything, came running after us with a bag on his shoulder. He politely asked whether he might be able to tell us something from his heart and if we didn't want to listen he would let us go. Obviously, we said yes.

Besides being a beach boy — which was just a way of getting by — he was studying film here in Cancún, and had a big exam coming up. He took some papers out of his bag — an ID card, some official-looking documents — and said that if he did well, he could get a scholarship to one of the best film schools in the United States, I think in Los Angeles or New York, I can't remember. Texas, maybe. Calmly, he told us about the exam, that he had to film a few tiny scenes of everyday life and he was supposed to play the lead role; it would take an hour tops. He just needed a few extras.

Lasse and I looked at each other and burst out laughing. 'Um, do we want to?' he said. 'No, of course we don't. Come on, Lasse,' I said. 'But don't you think Melanie would say yes?' he asked. Melanie was the coolest woman, about thirty years old, whom we had met on our trip and loved right away. She didn't have a job or a place to live, she did nothing but travel. We were just so fascinated by her life.

Then the boy said that of course he would understand if we were thinking, Why don't you just get some of your Mexican friends to help you, but they'd just make fun of him, whereas Europeans are way more open to this kind of thing and just get it when you have a passion for something. I smiled and said yes, what's the worst that could happen.

We followed him to the hotel on the other side of the road. It didn't look very inhabited, a large, cracked stone house with moisture in the walls, a little cold and desolate. I was actually pretty scared, but I didn't want to say anything to Lasse, so I just giggled a bit. But now I know that you should always trust your intuition, even when it's made of fear, because otherwise you might end up getting into a car headed somewhere strange. And even though you can't keep up — maybe you're still standing on the sidewalk — your body is in

52

the car, and then afterward, every time you're reminded of what happened, it feels like somebody else's bad feelings, but you're the one who has to feel them, you can never leave your body all the way. So, we followed the boy up to the third floor and into his room. He went out on the balcony and set up two white plastic chairs with a view of the ocean. I was relieved that we were supposed to sit out there because at least I could just jump off and get away if he turned out to be dangerous. The boy took out his camera and set it up on a chair inside the living room, to film me and Lasse through the sliding glass door.

The boy pressed record and got down in front of us on all fours. First, he was going to play the table, he said, we were just supposed to put our feet up on his back and talk about our time here in Mexico. We spoke in English while looking at the ocean. Afterward, he wanted to be a dog. He went behind the camera and said we should call him a dog's name — Tikki, I think it was — and then he came in on all fours and crawled around between our legs. We were supposed to act natural, to push him a little with our feet and keep talking. Then we were supposed to call him again and ask him to clean the floor. He came in with a wet rag and rubbed our feet too, the tiles were shining.

None of the scenes lasted more than two to four minutes, and after each one, he went back to the camera and told us what was going to happen next. Then he asked Lasse whether it was okay if he licked our feet, because that's what dogs do to clean them. 'Um, yeah,' said Lasse, and the boy started to crawl again. First he licked Lasse's feet, slowly up and down the arch of his foot, but when he got to me, it was like he was going to eat my whole foot! It was really warm and tickled between my toes. I couldn't stop laughing and couldn't stay in character. He gave Lasse the camera and asked if he wanted to give it a try. Next, I was supposed to walk him on a leash (made out of a T-shirt he had tied around his neck, I was supposed to hold the other end) and make him do things, dog things. He kept licking my toes and sucking them. I kept pulling my foot away and laughing to Lasse, though I couldn't see him behind the camera. The lens looked like a peephole in a metal door. Now the boy wanted me to use him like a table even though he was a dog. I was supposed to scold him and say all these mean things. 'Bad Mexican dog.' I tried to get into character, but he stopped me and said I should kick him harder and say that I didn't like Mexicans. I didn't want to do that, and I was on the brink of tears, so I said to Lasse, 'Babe, I can't do this anymore. Tell him we're done.' Lasse kept filming for a few seconds before he handed the camera to the boy and said we had to go, that the shot was probably good enough as it was. Lasse was about two heads taller than him and calmly laid a hand on his shoulder. The boy said thank you very much, and that he would come join us in two minutes for a cup of coffee.

We got out of there as fast as we could. Lasse was laughing and said it was nice to have such clean feet. I said I felt a bit violated and would rather not talk about it. In the lobby of our hotel, we ran into Melanie and actually didn't want to tell her about any of it, but I couldn't keep it inside, so I said to Lasse, 'Tell her what just happened to us.'

Melanie was totally shocked. She would never have done such a thing in her life!

Rachel, Nevada

And then she turned her cheek to him. Even before the train left the platform, she let her waving hand fall into her lap and stared at the empty seats of the compartment in front of her. He remained on the sun-bleached wooden platform off Nevada 375 and watched her disappear into the desert toward Alamo, and he said to himself: She is always in the company of loved ones. He was frustrated because, for almost seven years now, he had only been able to live in the loneliness of their daughters' absence. While she, even when alone and full of grief, always tried to be part of something. I'm really looking forward to being among mothers and daughters, she said back when she bought her ticket for the show. And as soon as the train started moving they were there with her, her face radiating the same light he knew from her daylong meditation sessions in the living room. A raving look of bliss would come over her, as if her organs were being replaced one at a time by small pieces of sunlit glass. She was eighty-three and you would have thought her bones were corroding.

Antonio's bones were corroding; at least that's how he felt, as if he had been lying dormant in this alkaline desert since the last ice age. He walked with slow, truncated steps, carefully lifting each foot to avoid tripping over a loose rock or the roots of a desiccated saltbush. His knee crackled and sent a dry stab of pain into his hip. With the highway at his back and the yellow setting sun in the corner of his right eye, he walked by the Little A'Le'Inn and past each of Rachel's forty-two homes, most of them mobile, which always made him think of the town as a kind of camp or settlement, somewhere that still bore traces of arrival. Six years ago, after they buried their daughters — who had both, within a year and a half, died of cancer — Fay and Antonio sold their apartment in Boston and bought a camper to drive across the country in. It was Fay's idea: If we're going to go on without them we need to figure out where to go, she said, pulling Antonio out of bed. He was depressed and afraid of falling asleep at the wheel, so she ended up driving most of the way, through Ohio, Indiana, Kansas, Colorado, until the road became itself a kind of sleep across the long stretches of Nevada desert. Something about Rachel, not so much its isolation as its peculiar and elastic time — which you could sense on the endless bush steppes and at the local UFO club where everyone, eager for new sightings, would mostly just *wait and see* — something about its protracted present had told them that they *had to pull over here*, that they had to spend their final years here. Fay went to the

Little A'Le'Inn and joined the club right away, and Antonio walked into the desert, as he was doing now. At the end of the gravel road, instead of going home to wait in their camper for Fay to return from the concert, he wedged a note in the mail slot and continued toward the dry steppe, which stretched dull brown from Bald Mountain, diagonally ahead, to the next mountain range twenty miles west. Out there, the mountains were black in their own shadows, the sky above them still orange between grey-purple clouds, and behind them, another steppe was flanked on both sides by mountains running parallel from north to south. The desert continued like that all the way to the Sierra Nevada, ribbed by streams and salt lakes but without any outlet to the ocean, reaching back to the Rocky Mountains five hundred miles to the east. The thought made Antonio dizzy and defiant, like the explorers who, in their journals, which he had read with enthusiasm, relentlessly rode through the desert in search of the Buenaventura River that was believed to cut across it. There was something unyielding about that image of the Great Basin, the wide-open desert devoid of a single trade route; it refused to settle in their brains.

He opened his eyes and didn't know he had sat down on the steppe. It was happening all the time lately — at any moment he could be drawn to the ground in a daze. A mineral darkness would bubble up inside him and begin to harden and crystallise. He got back up on his feet and shook the images out of his head, put Rachel farther behind him and turned on his flashlight. The soil was pale and rocky, sporadically covered in yellow straw, mugwort and snakeweed. It was silent, only the wind moving across the steppe, cold on his face and neck. Some nights, you could hear the small planes transporting military personnel to and from Area 51, another twelve miles into the desert. Or jet fighters in training broke the sound barrier, sending thunderous shock waves through the air. Occasionally, rays of light would shoot into the sky from LED flashlights in the hands of UFO enthusiasts signalling hope of contact. The truth was out there.

But not tonight. Antonio reached the foot of Bald Mountain and trudged up the first stretch to the rock formation that shot vertically into the sky, and continued along it, letting his fingers slide along the surface, smooth, fluted, jagged — the fossilised irregularities like an ancient collage. Some geologists had hypothesised that a meteor had struck the shallow expanse of water that covered the whole area a good 370 million years ago. The rock face broke off, and Antonio continued in the direction it pointed, down a hill and a few hundred yards ahead, where the ground began to drop into the darkness in front of him. Guided by the beam of his flashlight, he located the tarp at the edge of the lake, pried it loose and uncovered a car battery and a lime-green carry-on suitcase.

First, the lightning sound of electricity moving across a semi-vast distance, and then the dry lake was weakly illuminated by the lamps mounted on its shores. The lake bed a few yards below was level and white with salt deposited in layers. His hand on the suitcase, Antonio crawled down the small incline and set course for the Sender in the middle of the lake. The dark began to pulsate with crawling movements, and slowly individual organisms appeared. First, the scraggy creosote bushes that smelled like rain and should not have been this far north — the call of the Sender must have reached them by wind and made them wander up from the Mojave. Next, the mugwort and snakeweed and evergreen goosefoot, which usually kept to the edge of the lake. A few plants had reached all the way to the Sender, where the animals were as well. A matted fabric of fur and snouts, they writhed and rubbed themselves against one other: a mountain goat, three pronghorns and a herd of black-tailed jackrabbits, kangaroo rats, rabbits and other mammals, all nuzzling the Sender.

It had integrated all the forms of life that flocked to it, so completely that you could see it just by looking at the swarm of plants and animals. And as such, Antonio said to himself, the Sender was no more or less than the gathering it hosted. Still, he felt the urge to locate it under the fur, his gaze kept sliding upward, about five feet off the ground, where some of its surface was still visible between the lizards and reminded him of its dimensions: approximately two yards high and maybe half as wide, like a bale of hay, except parabolic on top. When he had discovered the Sender almost three years ago, its exterior — with the exception of a bulge it had acquired in its encounter with the desert soil — appeared perfectly whole and aerodynamic, crow-black and smooth, like an object meant to travel through the world oblivious to whatever matter it encountered. Now it was overgrown with a greenish-white fungus that had fused with its surface, making it spongy and porous. Its wound-like, almost breathing quality made you feel that you could stick your hand right through it — Antonio had tried once, and got to his knuckles. Below its outer, symbiotic layers, the Sender had perhaps retained some of its original metallic constitution.

But it was a willing metal. At the bottom it had given in to the animals' constant nuzzling and redistributed its mass so that there were small hollows and soft burrows that the rabbits and kangaroo rats curled up inside. Curlews and snipes had nested at the top, and at its base the metal had oozed into a trench containing just enough liquid for a cluster of fairy shrimp to hatch from their hibernation cysts.

When Antonio first discovered the Sender, while out hunting rabbits a little farther into the desert, he kept his hands off. It must have come from Area 51, fallout from some aborted flight testing, and he wasn't about to get involved in any of that. Whatever military exercises were conducted inside the barbed wire, they cared enough about keeping them secret to have ten uniformed men posted along a two-mile radius. Later that day, he sat with Fay at the Little A'Le'Inn, eating lunch before the weekly UFO club meeting. Should he tell her about the Sender? This was his chance to isolate her from the others — just the two of them in the desert, lonely, together — but she would probably insist that the discovery belonged to the club and everyone else searching for signs of alien life. So when she went to the meeting, he drove into the desert, hoisted the Sender into the back of their pickup truck and drove it carefully away from Area 51 to the dry lake at the foot of Bald Mountain. Five days later he returned, and when he reached the top of the hill and saw the Sender surrounded by birds and mammals, he screamed. And he watched how the animals tensed and hovered for a second above the white lake bed.

He heard his own cry resonate with the call emitted by the Sender: a dark and clear metallic dissonance. With horror and pleasure, he felt an amorphous desert life unfold inside him with tectonic slowness. Then the animals fell to the ground and resumed their rubbing against the Sender. He imagined that it had been sent from Area 51 into space to attract alien creatures with its cry, but instead had crashed and was now calling out to the aliens of the earth: the waders, marsupials, wild rabbits and horned ruminants, ancient species with memories from before the earth was peopled. But it didn't matter to him where the Sender had come from or why — all theories seemed irrelevant. Deep in his lungs he could still feel the scream that had just been in his throat, and that the Sender screamed without pause. And he felt the foreign life, simultaneously inside him and swelling in full daylight on the lake bed. It was as if the feeling he had had since their daughters' death, of being completely isolated from everyone, had found its voice and finally become a thing in itself, a breathless, metallic longing. He had to become the Sender.

Now, three years later, he was finally ready to go through with the operation. Five yards from the Sender, he parked the lime-green suitcase, unzipped it and arranged his implements: the scalpels, mouthpiece and spoons; they quivered with the sound of the scream. Fay was probably winding through the mountains that wrapped around Las Vegas to the north, he thought, following the train's likely progress on a map in his head. What was she looking at right now? The closer he came to the transformation, the more he wished, the more concentratedly he prayed, that she would know what he was up to, even now on the train, before she returned home and found his note in the mail slot. He was so afraid of losing himself that he could only do it if he imagined her there holding his hand. And at the same time, he needed to be alone to come out here and do it. It had been like that since their daughters had passed away – he needed so badly to be alone, ideally somewhere deserted, and as soon as he was, he missed Fay and wanted her to be there with him. She had always seemed so calm and fearless in their relationship, as if she didn't have any sense of being-an-I that could be destroyed. It was the same humility with which she met other people, like when they first settled down in Rachel. She had never been interested in aliens before; nevertheless, she started going to the Little A'Le'Inn, listening to people's stories without judgment, participating in the weekly meetings and excursions of the UFO club, even studying the representation of extraterrestriality in Western popular culture on her own. You shouldn't dismiss the actuality of these myths, she would say to Antonio when he couldn't muster more than a laugh at *that freak show*, sad and frustrated to be spending yet another night alone in the camper while she was in the desert with them. He couldn't help feeling that she was being unfaithful to him and their grief. But it's all just business and projection, he would say, citing, for example, Ted Riddle, the owner of the Little A'Le'Inn, who in his own words started believing in aliens when he realised they were good for business, but also imagined them floating in collusion with the Feds and the UN, part of a conspiracy to take away good citizens' right to bear arms, and that's how they were preparing for the alien invasion, *simply selling the planet.*

Or Antonio would cite the numerous unemployed priests in the area who had suddenly become mediums for life forms from other solar systems. Or the self-proclaimed ufologists who numbered a good half of Rachel's fifty-six residents, including Ted Riddle's son Chris, who investigated the various cases of animal mutilation that occurred in the area. Horse and cattle corpses were found with their eyes, tongues and genitals cut off. In many cases, the rectum had also been removed with a razor-sharp hexagonal plug that had been driven into the animal's asshole and ripped out with gut and flesh. Or the spine and the brain might be missing, it varied from case to case, as if someone or something was collecting the various parts necessary to recreate our species on their own planets, was Chris's theory. And a lot points back to him, Antonio said. Think about how he's always finding those animals before the ranchers, or that he's just coincidentally around the corner whenever they call — he's obviously *the one mutilating those animals*, but no one else sees it, because the prime suspect is some Scandinavian-type alien. In Chris's case, thought Antonio, UFOs were a distant fiction that gave him license to commit these crimes, and even to make money off them, in the form of the beautiful, impressionistic identikits that he painted and exhibited at his dad's bar. Wow, Fay said with a drawn-out sigh, you really don't believe in other people's belief, do you? Haven't you noticed how people here, honest folks like Ted Riddle and myself, are staying up all night, staring at the sky and listening to radio signals? Haven't you noticed the people painting and writing books and making music about aliens? They're doing so much more than the bare minimum.

Besides, all of the tourists nowadays want to see proof before they get here. And so it's nice that we actually *do see* things, she said, and started listing the sightings she had been part of: an indefinable ray of light with a colour and intensity that couldn't have reached her from the stars; an object flying in bizarre fits and spurts across the sky, with none of the smooth continuity characteristic of human technology; and then again, a few months ago, another one of those unlikely plane crashes that seemed to occur around Rachel every six months. Each time, military personnel were at the crash site within a few minutes, quarantining the area, vacuuming the ground of wreckage for a day or two.

Antonio opened his eyes with a start at having fallen asleep, looked down at himself and all around him, as if someone had been there and done something to him while he slept. Everything was the same as before, the lake bed golden white in the lamplight, and the bushes stretched out, reaching their roots toward the Sender. The animals nuzzled against it in their strangely patient way, quiet with the exception of their furry breath. He understood the people who believed that they had been zapped by aliens and subjected to experiments or sexual abuse. That alarming sensation of a rupture in continuity, having taken place without one's knowledge, like waking up behind the wheel of a car about to collide with another car. Or the endangered elephants awakening groggy on a television show with chains around their necks. If anyone believed in aliens, it had to be those elephants. Antonio got to his feet and shook the images out of his head. It was time. Fay was probably standing in the concert hall among mothers and daughters, waiting for Karen Ruthio, 'The Wandering Woman of the Desert States', to come on. He set the suitcase upright, spread a paper tablecloth over it and laid out the implements in front of his right hand. The scalpels lay there, looking indifferent to the pain they were about to inflict. That's what he told himself as he grasped the largest one. That to the metal it wouldn't be violent, merely an encounter with a softer and more viscous material. He broke out in a cold sweat and trembled in all of his muscles. Of course his body would resist, but he couldn't deal with that now. If he was going to go through with the operation, he needed to do so by willing himself into a state that he could now only perceive as a threat. The transformation demanded that he put himself at a distance, he understood, that he disregard his body. With the index and middle finger of his left hand he located the two hard rings of cartilage right beneath his larynx, stretched the skin taut between them and made a horizontal incision. The skin opened with a slight delay, as if it first had to realise it had been sliced, and then came the blood and pain, sweet, acidic, warm. He tasted it as much as he felt it in his nerves. With a slightly smaller scalpel, he deepened the incision, working through the layers of skin, through the blood vessels and fatty tissue, while he held the wound open with a spoon in his left hand. The pain shot through his throat in fiery rays. But even if he imagined that his flesh belonged to someone else, there was still something impossible about manoeuvring the knife, something unreal about the measured motions through layer after layer of human flesh. Almost in sync with his working hands, he had to reach for something to come, with an open hand like when you want to touch the rain, and summon all his courage from there. It felt like leaving the task in someone else's hands. Suddenly his windpipe popped out of the wet flesh, distended and fluted with cartilage.

Feeling his own breathing flow against his index finger through a thin wall — combined with the almost electric pain in his severed nerve endings — filled him with an animate nausea, an appetite he hadn't felt since he was young. Wind passed through the open wound, thick as water.

He raised his head and looked at the Sender, just like Fay and the others in the audience were looking at Karen Ruthio — how was a voice like that coming out of a seventy-nine-year-old woman? The scream was still a mystery to him, that dark, metallic tone that sounded like dissonance in itself, as if it were out of tune with the world. He hadn't been able to scream that scream since that day almost three years ago when it suddenly quivered inside his throat. Not because it was outside the range of his vocal cords, but because it was located somewhere in the depth between two frequencies, a secret gap that broke with the mathematical principles they had always followed. One day, almost a year ago, after screaming at the Sender for hours, he squeezed himself between the mammals and laid his forehead against it. Through its outer, fungal layers he felt a weak vibration, deep and metallic like the scream, and suddenly knew that he needed to have some of it inside him. That the scream could only be produced by the specific composition of the Sender, which was both malleable and very hard. With his angle grinder, he had sliced off a small piece, squeezing his eyes shut at the brightness of the crystals that appeared at the incision site: half an inch in diameter, glowing clear green and citrus yellow, the likely result of a very slow cooling process. Something about the way the material liquefied above the Bunsen burner – the way the particles collectively yielded their solid form, as it changed from grey-purple to orange to smouldering sun yellow – made him think that the heating up was a kind of overture, that he was caressing the material with the flame, just like the animals were nestling against it, that it let itself be melted down, because it had been touched with a tenderness that exceeded the bonds of its atoms. That's the grace of all things, he thought, or for a moment sensed at the edges of his consciousness and, blinking, forgot again.

Now the mouthpiece lay ready on the operating table: one and a half inches long and one inch in diameter, it came to a point at a fifteen-degree angle. The new crystals were not visible, but the material still retained some of the greenish sheen to which he attributed its ability to bond to other forms of life. He leaned his head back, located the two rings of cartilage beneath his larynx and cut a small entry to the windpipe between them. Leading with the narrow end, he pushed the mouthpiece in, and exhaled so his vocal cords gaped open. He felt the mouthpiece slide through the opening, then made a noise with the last of his exhalation so that his vocal cords tensed around it, holding it tightly in their V. Lastly, he mounted the respiration band: an eight-inch-long section of flexible plastic tubing, one end in his mouth and the other in the hole at his larynx.

The mouthpiece was cold and hard and way too smooth for the mucous environment of his throat. He could feel his own vocal cords down there too, small reptiles rubbing against the instrument. He looked up at the Sender, listening to it, to the cry that radiated green through the fungus, the lizards, the scraggy mammals and plants, and bound them together in a drawn-out, mystical labour. Its meaning was hidden to him, but if he could transform himself into the Sender, if he could produce the Sender's cry in his own throat, he would produce its meaning inside himself and so become part of the ritual. Tensing his lungs and throat as much as possible, he screamed, and then screamed again with a little less force, trying in any way possible to express the feeling in his stomach, but mustered only a cough. The salt deposits lay like ancient puzzle pieces on the lake bed, which made him think about how the lake had both evaporated and drained into itself, how the whole desert was a massive basin emptying itself out like that, up into the sky and down through its base. He thought about the humility and zeal of that movement as he screamed again. After a few minutes, the mouthpiece began to vibrate in his throat. With varying force, he repeated the movement until a sound reverberated and the animals around the Sender stopped to listen. The scream swelled as much from his own mouth as back through his windpipe and down into his belly, where it was making his organs oscillate, a pitch-black dissonance that made it impossible for him to think of the cry as an expression of his loneliness or anything else inside him. It was more like someone or something was stimulating his throat into speaking, and as a side effect, was activating the memory of a distant, desert life.

Antonio inhaled and accidentally broke the stream of air that sustained the scream. The animals turned back to the

Sender and resumed their nuzzling overtures. The respiratory band was working well, though. Air flowed from his mouth into the plastic tube that led back into his windpipe beneath his larynx, and it would have probably continued if he hadn't got in the way. If he could only abandon his breathing, that eternal preparation. You take a deep breath to get ready for what's to come, just like in the UFO club, where you couldn't do more than wait and prepare. But he was tired of the waiting and wanted to enter the present. He wanted to create a streaming band of respiration — the continuous scream — inside himself. He envied Fay her belief. He had realised it six months earlier, up at the Little A'Le'Inn, during the last of her six lectures on aliens in the history of film. He was seated in the back of the room, admiring her above the heads of the members of the UFO club. It was strange and beautiful, sixty-one years into their marriage, to see her standing in front of the screen, with the remote control calmly resting in her left hand changing the slides in time with her speech, the complex and supple language that she had acquired over the course of her studies, and which she was now speaking with an ease that made a long academic career unfold out of a past she must have been living in parallel to the life they had lived together. Over the course of the last five Tuesdays, she had, through comparative readings of selected biblical passages and the most important films of the past sixty years about encounters with extraterrestrial life, put forth her theory that aliens signified the return of the Judeo-Christian God in Western popular culture. The key motifs in the representation of alien intelligence could all be correlated to specific biblical revelations, and the cinematic development of the alien-image roughly corresponded to the shift from the Old to the New Testament God, from the almighty, unpredictable aliens, punishing from above, to those who, in some biological form, had made their dwellings among humans and had to play by earthly rules. But for some reason everyone has skipped Paul, said Fay, and turned off the projector. Silence fell over the Little A'Le'Inn. Only the wheezing of the oldest members of the audience was audible. The overhead lights turned on, Fay squinted. It is no longer I who live, but Christ who lives in me. Why haven't any of the sci-fi screenwriters read Paul? She looked out into the room and let her arms fall to her sides, sinking a bit into herself in front of the screen. I know I haven't been here for as long as many of you. But what I've seen in this town, I have no doubt that it's faith. I know that we're waiting for spaceships just like we're waiting for the Saviour. And I know that those of you still working are praying that they'll come and keep your businesses afloat. Just like you prayed you would hit a new vein in the mines when they were about to close. And what were we offered instead? New lights in the sky! Antonio watched her with a mixture of envy and shame at envying her her faith, as if it were something she owned. But it gave her something that he didn't have; namely, the possibility of living with things that were as if they were nothing, or the other way around. Just as her belief that the souls of the dead were stored like information in the atmosphere made it possible for her — through long fasts and rituals that were supposed to open her up to cosmic radiation — to receive their daughters inside her, however transient and painful that might be.

Maybe it was also possible because she had known them before they were born, and felt their bodies as a part of her own when she carried them, nursed them and bathed them, and since then, everything she had done with them had added to that feeling, filling the same place in her body, which had become empty and open when they died. To Antonio, they were gone, or in the best case existed in a realm that he could never access because he couldn't believe in it, and it felt like a humiliation. It was humiliating to accept their definitive absence, but it was the only way he knew how to grieve: in solitude, like the residue left behind when they no longer existed in their own particular ways, but had fallen back into something dead and formless in the earth. Sometimes it felt like there wasn't anything left for him to do on Earth. It was a demeaning form of consolation to call their phones, whose plans he had secretly kept paying, to listen to their voicemail greetings, at once so unreal in the breathless telephone receiver and corporeal with the sounds of their moving tongues and mouths, amplified by the microphone's compressor. Fay concluded her presentation by suggesting an *authentication of faith*, an acknowledgment that aliens could manifest in here as well as out there, which over the next few months radically changed the practice of the UFO club. They started to supplement their sender and receiver equipment with a kind of spiritual technology, rituals in which each person renounced parts of themselves in the form of secrets, possessions, hair, nails, teeth and blood, and intimate visions of the coming life forms. With these rituals, they generated a kind of communal energy, capable of attracting aliens in the night, and at the same time made space in themselves to receive them. At first, this had a calming effect, fostering trust among the members of the UFO club and in Rachel in general. The sense of space-ships as a looming danger or part of a cosmic-federal conspir-acy ran slowly out into the sand. But then a new nervousness started to quiver in town, as if the aliens, finally torn loose from their earthly conceptions — and especially from Area 51, lurking south of Bald Mountain — had once more taken on the violent potential of *something*, something that didn't yet have a name or shape, but that you still, or maybe exactly for that reason, needed to prepare for. Ted Riddle stopped foisting monitoring equipment and badges onto UFO tourists because he *honestly didn't know* whether the aliens were correctly de-picted, or whether they even emitted radiation that would reg-ister on the electromagnetic spectrum. He carved the bar logo with its stereotypical grey, pupil-less alien out of the wooden sign along the highway, leaving behind a hole into the desert. The ufologists abandoned their theories and instead read the Letters of Paul aloud when they were sought out by tourists with accounts of paranormal activity. The residents of Rachel started to switch off the water supply and electricity in their mobile homes in the morning, break down their beds, reel in their awnings and repeat the whole process in reverse before bed. People developed a nervous relationship with their daily routines. Even the elderly, who were the majority, ran fran-tically around, fumbling their things in a state of nervous excitement that might seem almost pubescent except that it was soothed by a kind of shared impotence, a hesitation in all their desires. Hands had second thoughts on their way toward

74

spouses' hips or hands, toward grabbing their coffee cups at the Little A'Le'Inn. Feet left accelerators and let cars roll to a stop on the highway, on the way to the monthly shopping trip in Alamo. Should you dust off your camper, sweep the branches off the road, should you even shower today? There were flickers in the sky, meteoric red and yellow lights, and clear white light that moved in inhuman stutters, but only a few of them were filmed and business suffered, people gained and lost weight all at once.

Antonio awoke almost choking on his own breathing. The pain burned sour in his throat. Coughing made the plastic tube writhe in the wound. He took it out of his mouth, leaned his head back and opened the passageway. Then he got back up on his legs and shook the images out of his head, images of jackrabbits with long, erect ears and black-spotted coats. Hundreds of jackrabbits hopping across the steppes, dry lakes and mountainsides, the jackrabbit being a kind of totem animal in Karen Ruthio's universe – the images were being sent to him from Las Vegas! He had read about her concerts, that she sometimes, toward the end of the show, would ask the audience who they were missing, who was alone somewhere and needed a greeting. She would choose one person from the many who had their hands in the air, because *we'll need all of our psychic energy*, as she had said in the article. Antonio Simmons is in Rachel, Nevada, she was saying now, while the band played the first few bars of "Strong Legs, Attentive Ears". In a moment you'll see an image on the screen. I am going to sing about this image. And you are going to send it to Antonio Simmons. He is lying asleep in Rachel, Nevada.

He will dream about this image. Try to send it to him. And on the screen a black-tailed jackrabbit appeared, and Karen Ruthio sang, *Jackrabbit, jackrabbit — always on the run / I see you running parallel to my prayers across the steppe* ... Antonio exhaled and felt the metal begin to oscillate; it was still warm. The scream emerged in his throat and harmonised with the Sender's scream above the lake. It was inside him now, a distant, matt-red desert full of terrestrial organisms, but still empty and differently vast from this desert, or at least the images the scream evoked inside him were. Maybe they were of the desert as it would look without him there. And then his breathing got in the way and blew it to pieces, and he wanted to choke his breathing. Even in the most deserted places, he heard the sound of his own heart and his lungs, those stubborn factories. Their incessant activity was like a promise of a way out or a purpose he had to let go of. It was a slow and painful realisation. That he needed to let go of the thought of sharing his coming union with the Sender and the plants and the animals with Fay. But it meant everything to him now, the possibility that she would find his note in the mail slot, rush out here and find him screaming with the animals nuzzling around him. And she would take his hand and become part of the ritual.

But to leave his breathing behind and enter the now was to eliminate the distance between himself and the next moment, and thereby to lose the future. And all of his conceptions, all his hope and fear and courage, came from the future.

He had to lose that which only in the moment of loss would stop meaning everything.

He didn't understand. And then he did it.

He made the mouthpiece vibrate, and as the air seeped out of his lungs he listened to the monotone dissonance of the scream, received what it promised, felt it spread through his breast and make his organs oscillate so that a formless life gushed forth — and after a moment's silence at the end of his exhale, the scream turned him into pure vibration. Air streamed through the respiratory band, from his mouth and back into the tube beneath his larynx, a perfect, circular continuity whose sound was the scream. Around the Sender, the animals stiffened as if they were receiving two conflicting commands. The snipes flapped, bewildered, and the plants trembled on the lake bed. Some of the mammals withdrew from the mass of fur and made their way, as if in a trance, to Antonio, and pressed against him. Two pronghorns, a lynx, a number of jackrabbits and wild rabbits; they found their places among each other and started to nuzzle his legs and groin. The birds landed on his shoulders, lizards leaped from the antelopes to his chest and pressed their bellies against him. But he was full to his skin with the vibration of the scream and couldn't feel them. It made his contours flicker in the crystal-green light that was itself the encounter between his body and the animals'. There was only their union, and not his feeling of joy that it was finally happening. There was only joy. Diagonally across, the Sender quivered in perfect symmetry with him. The light that streamed from them collided in a wall of green spirals.

A vehicle wheezed somewhere in the desert, quickly approaching. As two white beams of light fell over the lake, the sound of the motor forced its way through the vibration and into Antonio. With a long gasp he inhaled, breaking the respiratory band, and the scream faded in his throat. Warmth returned to his body, blood rushed into his face and hands. He felt the animals leave him, and blinked. The vehicle came to a stop at the edge of the lake, doors opened, hurried steps approached from the left on the crunchy ground. Twenty yards away, they came into view, backlit by the vehicle: twelve uniformed men with their rifles aimed at him. Don't shoot, cried Antonio, but only a dry whistle came out. All his strength had left him. His bones rattled and pulled him toward the lake bed. He wanted to tell them that the Sender was theirs, that he wouldn't say anything to anyone if they just let him go. He was only thinking of Fay now, and almost falling apart at the thought of not seeing her again. He's ancient, hissed one of the soldiers. Antonio looked at him pleadingly and sat down next to the suitcase. Somewhere above their heads, something was moving in the air, but its buzzing was different from the fighter jets and commercial planes, not as piercing. A small, pitch-black circle appeared in the sky and grew larger in fits and spurts. Fifty or a hundred yards away, as Antonio began to be able to make out its enormous egg-shaped dimensions, it turned onto its side, and decelerated as it approached. In the middle of the black circle, parallel with its rounded sides, a golden, oval band emerged, its beam so bright that it eclipsed the headlights of the military vehicle. I don't know them! Antonio shouted. It's got nothing to do with me. But the soldiers had already turned their guns toward the flying object. It came to a stop in the air ten yards above their heads, where it hovered, glistening like a cosmic reflection of the lake bed.

The animals seemed afraid or expectant, clinging to the Sender, which was located underneath the centre of the object. It was difficult to see in the bright light, but Antonio thought that he could discern a furrowed, granite texture. He heard a dozen bullets penetrating rock before a viscous light emerged from the oval band.

The soldiers went blurry, their guns sounded distant and irrelevant. The projectiles lost speed and dropped in the full white light. It hovered, billowing like a cloak under water, a curtain between two ages, encircling Antonio and the plants and animals. Inside there was only the scream, which was no longer dissonant. The animals pressed against the Sender, Antonio pressed against them. He could feel the earth beneath them shaking and breaking loose from the rest of the lake bed. Above their heads, the underside of the flying object transformed into an oval entryway, full of the same crystal-green light coming from the Sender, which just a few minutes ago had also come from Antonio. Now they were being sucked into it along with the loosened ground beneath them, while the air became thicker, pressing on his lungs. The oval grew and flooded his vision. The plants and animals were washed out in the light; that was now all there was: a blinding green, viscous light emitted from somewhere deeper inside, and the mouthpiece throbbing excitedly in his throat.

He woke full of fear and gasped for air. His skeleton ached like it might collapse into a pile of bones at any moment. The wound at the base of his throat had been closed with a barely perceptible suture — it felt like his skin had been melted, spread over the incision site and left to congeal — but he could still feel the empty space where the mouthpiece had been. He coughed and it tasted like desert. When he turned his head a little to the left, he could make out the few lights still on in Rachel, and to the right, the first few yards of the desert slipping into darkness. He got back up on his legs and shook the images out of his head, set course for their camper a few hundred yards away. It was two o'clock in the morning; Fay was probably on the train somewhere between Rachel and Alamo. It was quiet, no sound or light in the sky or in the desert behind him, but he hurried anyway, pushing his legs forward with his weight, waddling away with pain radiating through his bones.

Finally home in the camper, he collapsed into his armchair. He woke up again when Fay walked through the door. The skin around her eyes was heavy and dark with fatigue, but she was radiant, her thin, copper-coloured hair sticking out in all directions. Antonio fought his way out of the chair to embrace her. I met her! she said, overjoyed, before he reached her in the kitchen. Who? he asked. Karen Ruthio! said Fay, stretching out her arms. She came to me, at one point she got off the stage and came to me in the audience. 'Finally, I see you,' she said, and looked me in the eye. 'Yes,' I said, but did she know who I was? 'Yes, we've met before,' she said. 'When?' I asked. 'We've met on the radio.' She really said that, Antonio! We met on the radio!

KAREN RUTHIO
b. Gold Hill, Nevada, 1928—d. Route 95
in Esmeralda County, Nevada, 2017

American singer-songwriter and accordionist, known for her music about life in and between American mining towns in the twentieth century.

As the daughter, and later the wife, of a mine worker, in the majority of her albums Ruthio deals with experiences of a life lived in motion between temporary stints of work in the mines. The title track of her debut album, *Dragged Through the Desert* (1967), at nine minutes long, is an arrhythmical composition of violins, claves, accordions and Ruthio's dark voice, which unfolds the image of a woman on a horse with a child on her back. The woman isn't unfamiliar with this horse, but also doesn't seem to be in control of it; she isn't riding it so much as she is being pulled along, just as the horse is being pulled along; with a rope, it is tied to another horse, ridden by the woman's husband, which seems to set their tempo and course through the desert. But it turns out that the husband's horse is being pulled by a third horse, which is trotting even farther ahead, and so the caravan continues endlessly, the horses alternately occupied by women with children and men bearing substantial loads, and bound together by a white rope, which ends in 'a hole in the earth, owned by a liar.' The pit glistens with copper as it draws the sun and the rope into it.

Other tracks cast settled, small-town life in a nomadic light: housekeeping is revealed to be an illusion, cleaning a futile guard against the desert dust and the husband who incessantly comes home dirty from the mines; the kitchen table becomes an attempt to 'empty dinner of dirt' and 'lift your meals up into the sky'; teaching the girls to do house-work, as well as sending the boys off with their fathers to the mines, is like passing down a burdensome skill. A number of Karen Ruthio's songs are about a woman who wakes at night and goes outside to fall asleep again on the cold ground, or to wander around 'the comic labyrinth of the town' until she knows it well enough to do it with her eyes closed, and to 'reinscribe it in sleep'. Most of the time, the songs end with her leaving Earth in a spaceship or dreaming about doing so. Occasionally, other women come out and walk alongside her, and in "Woman Walks Home at Night (version 8)", it has become common practice: every night, all of the women of the town sleepwalk between the houses, discussing the town constitution, its norms and laws and their daily lives, 'settling down over and over again'.

Even though she was already writing songs at the age of twelve in Tonopah, Nevada, after inheriting an accordion from her father, Karen Ruthio didn't release her first album until she was thirty-nine. At that point, she was living with her husband, Henry Colberg, and their four children in Ruth, which was one of the few towns in Nevada to enjoy a relatively stable mining sector through the latter half of the twentieth century; for the first time in Karen's life, it was possible to settle down for more than a few years. It was in Ruth that she first met the women who would eventually make up her band, and in Ruth that she saved up enough money to record their first three albums: in addition to the aforementioned debut from 1967, *Reclaiming the Salt* (1968) and *Open-Pit Mining* (1972). Thanks to their traditional instrumentation (violin, upright bass, upright piano, hammer dulcimer, spoons, etc.) and limited distribution — primarily at gas stations and roadside joints in Utah and Nevada — the albums received almost no critical attention but found a devoted fanbase in the neighbouring suburbs, where Karen Ruthio started to be hired to play at annual town fairs. Proceeds from the shows went to the construction of a school in Ruth, and to keeping the town's last mine afloat after the Kennecott Copper Corporation pulled out in 1977 due to falling copper prices. A year and a half later, the band's local popularity started to peter out, or at least the other towns in White Pine County, all in danger of going bankrupt, could no longer afford to pay them. The mines yielded only small quantities of copper and were eventually closed in November '78. The members of the band dispersed across the desert with their husbands, pulled to the few operational mines left in Nevada, Utah, Arizona.

Karen Ruthio and Henry Colberg moved to Austin, Nevada. Founded during the silver rush of 1862 — which reportedly erupted when a Pony Express horse kicked a rock aside — and abandoned by the thousands when the precious metal supply ran out, Austin had, by 1978, become a living ghost town with about a hundred residents. Houses, hotels and churches stood empty in various stages of disrepair. A small corner of town was kept afloat by a minimal amount of turquoise extraction. Henry found work in the mines, Karen made jewellery out of the supple mineral, their youngest son moved away. She was writing songs, but couldn't afford to record them, and she didn't want to without her band. She walked around town missing her friends. A mile east, there was a squat granite tower, which she occasionally climbed to play music in. In the summer of 1982, this resulted in her album *Black-Tailed Jackrabbit*, largely instrumental, recorded with a dictaphone and released in 2001 in bootleg. Long, chromatic stretches of accordion improvisation, which occasionally take the form of composed music, ring hard and sacrosanct in the high-ceilinged room on the third floor of the tower. The granite becomes a second voice. The echo of the room amplifies the sound of Ruthio's movements on the chair and the sound of the chair being moved across the hard floor. You can hear her coughing and clearing her throat, and once in a while she sings a bit — sparse lines about longing and loneliness, about not having anyone to share her thoughts with, about the pain of having to read Hegel on her own. (The women of Ruth met weekly to discuss the literature and philosophy that they weren't able to read with their spouses. While the boys became men at an early age and started working in the mines, many of the women of the town had gone to school, played an active role in their children's education and eventually developed an inclination for novels and philosophical treatises, which they purchased collectively by mail order from Los Angeles. Typical readings included Southern Gothic novels and works of German idealism.) Six times over the course of the record, she invokes the black-tailed jackrabbit: three times in the form of sober descriptions of its physical characteristics and breeding habits; once as 'mother'; once as 'a meal of grandmothers';

and finally, as the 'attentive ears' that will deliver an important message to longed-for friends.

Over the next ten years, Karen Ruthio lived in four different places in Nevada and Arizona, saved up and didn't write any songs. In 1994, Henry passed away.

During the next few months, she managed to track down her old band members, almost all of them now widowed. In June of 1995, they gathered in Bonnie Claire, Nevada, ghost town since '54, but still supplied with electricity and running water, and crucially located at the last exit on Route 95 before Las Vegas. The band renovated the old hotel in town, with a café in the foyer, a practice space in the dining room, and a room for each of them on the second floor. One of the people who stopped by the café and had a Karen Ruthio album thrust into his hands was Robert Doxey, *Los Angeles Times* music critic, who, after listening to *Reclaiming the Salt*, thought to himself: This is exactly what I've been looking for. It's nothing like what I've been looking for. In a series published in the paper in March, April and May of '97, he dubbed Karen Ruthio 'Neil Young's long-lost sister' and 'country's answer to Laurie Anderson: The mother of art-country.' None of the labels stuck.

This coverage prompted the rerelease of Ruthio's first three albums from her time in Ruth, and a short-lived blast of attention, which peaked at a mediocre show at SXSW in '99. Over the course of the next few years, however, Ruthio found a solid following in Utah, Colorado, Arizona and Nevada, primarily among women who lived in small desert towns or hailed from them, women from farming and mining families and those women's children. With the money coming in from now-regular concerts in Las Vegas, Phoenix and Salt Lake City, the band built a recording studio in the basement of the Bonnie Claire Hotel, and from 2002 to 2009, another three albums saw the light of day. *Inhabiting Ghost Towns* (2002) tells the story of a town that has to be transported a hundred yards down a mountain to make room for the expansion of an open silver mine on the city limits, told over two unbroken, ambient compositions. *Ark* (2004) features ten pop songs about various plant and animal species native to the Bonnie Claire area and one about a spaceship that comes to pick them up. And finally, *OreCore* (2009) revolves around a cult, the worshippers of the 'Sun-Sun': the prophesied union of the sun and the fiery core of the earth, which the cult has been tasked to accelerate and prepare. They travel around, levelling houses, churches and crosses into the ground, 'turning all erect edifices to dust'. They settle down and dig large holes, extracting and selling precious metals. The cult is rich, but they live a primitive lifestyle, sleeping on the ground (*sun on my belly, sun on my back / and inside me the Sun-Sun's chamber / The black flames of the plague in the manger*) — all of their profits go to the development of digging and pumping technologies. Many are sacrificed along the way. The album's long, monotone tracks and twelve-tone interludes drag with their heavy and distorted instrumentation, but Ruthio's dark voice seems to drive them forward, making it difficult to discern pessimism from hope, productivity from ruin.

Karen Ruthio didn't write any more songs after 2009, but she played live shows to the very end: 'My veins may be all dried up, but my throat sure isn't', as she told a journalist in October 2015. Death took her by surprise two years later in the back of a tour bus.

Me, Rory and Aurora

It was me, Rory and Aurora, back then they lived in a flat smack up against the tracks. Crawling back and forth between their living room and bedroom was like taking the train, Rory had punched a big angry hole in the wall one day while Aurora was at church, like the tunnel on that train line. Well, one day Rory said he didn't love Aurora anymore, and looked at me with eyes I think I'd call turned around, I mean they were looking as much into his own brain as at me, and seeking affirmation in both places. I said why and didn't feel like talking about it when she wasn't home, and in a way I was their child, so how was I supposed to talk to him about it anyway? My main interest, besides running away with Aurora, and I would never get her to agree to that, was to keep being their kid. She's always out and about, he said, she's not interested in *our* life anymore. Kiss my ass, I said, and went to bed with a rancid taste in my mouth because of what his *our* implied, that something like a his-and-my life could exist without her.

Luckily she came home and threw her puffy jacket on the floor. I could tell from the sound of fabric collapsing and the way she sighed, a drawn-out, useless whistle like electric signals moving through a burnt-out computer. Where have you been? Rory asked. At the church, Aurora said. What'd you make? Enough, she said, and dumped all the money on the table in the kitchen, where he was making leek soup. I could smell it by the sweet, oniony steam seeping toward me in bed. The room was nearly dark, bundles of warm light poked through the hole in the wall. Headlights slid over the ceiling that was shaking from the trains. Does it really take all day to sell your shit to the faithful? Rory said. Does it take all day to steal vegetables for your soup? Aurora replied. Who's the one with a baby in their belly? I was lying halfway down the gap between the two mattresses, my shoulder blades against the wooden pallet, which I had found out walking one day and dragged back home — like how a cat brings in dead birds, Rory had said, and it was fair enough: I was quiet and cuddly and almost never in the way, I registered everything that happened in the flat. A little food was all I needed but I could easily go a day or two without. And every once in a while I'd come home, guilty and proud, with some sort of junk they hadn't asked for but had to accept: a wooden pallet, a board game, a lump of amber. Ceramic shoulder pads Rory would put on when he got drunk. There wasn't any shame in letting them take care of me, it was hot and sometimes turned us on, but it would have hurt if I couldn't return the favour.

Later — I must have been sleeping — they got into bed all stiff and stubborn with the silence they brought with them from the kitchen table. The air grew hard between their shoulders where I was curled up, and then Rory turned onto his side and snuggled up to Aurora, saying hey or babe or some other conciliatory thing. I wanted to join in as usual, to wedge myself between their laps and start on both of them while they kissed, but it was their fight and I guess their make-up too. I wriggled to the foot of the bed, crawled out and lay down under the pallet. Rory rolled onto his back again, his bony body closing the gap between the mattresses. He pulled his buttocks that were above my chest up and away from me as his shoulder blades pushed against the pallet, so his lower back became an arched bridge of skin. It smelled like sweat loosening the dirt he had accumulated during the day.

And then it was Aurora on her belly between the mattresses, pressed softly against the crisscrossed planks. I laid the palm of my hand against one of them and could vaguely feel the weight of her belly through it. Involuntarily, and with a sense of irritation that exceeded the tenderness, I felt for a second entirely equal with the creature on the other side of the wood and the belly skin and whatever else was shielding it from me. Dropped into this cramped flat, it would have to find its place in Rory and Aurora's life, between the furniture and piles of clothes, the way they'd been living for a while. Who knew why that baby had chosen to come here. Who knew whether the world you were in before you let yourself be sucked into conception was as barren and formless and freezing cold as mine had been the night I met Rory and Aurora at that bar eight months earlier. They were out drinking up the last of her redundancy pay, celebrating her return from rehab, Rory was glowing. I had gone out hoping someone would buy me drinks and offer me cigarettes, and they did. They told me about their lives, that they had moved to London because Aurora got a job as a teacher at a local school, which she lost soon after when she lost their child in the sixth month and went to the dogs, and I loved sitting there hearing about it. I loved the lack that was so clearly part of their lives, since they were babbling about it to a stranger between giggles that made their martinis spill. It was paranoid and hot how they were getting closer on both sides. I followed them home because I was hungry. The sex and fun we had was so good that they let me stay, or maybe they were just sympathetic to my situation. Or maybe they were sympathetic *because* we had such a good time together, so in that sense I also invested some of my personality that night. I followed them because I was hungry. Next thing I was in love with Aurora.

Now I was climbing back into bed and falling asleep to her breath. Her hand on my shoulder shook me awake, did I want to come with her? Rory was still sleeping.

She preferred to work alone, probably knowing that we would never really do anything without her, so it felt special to be brought along. Sitting across from her on the train going backwards, watching things disappear. A timid streaming orange light in the leaves and the rails and the rail workers' bodies, like they hadn't returned to themselves after sleep. Their hammering sounded daring and impossible so early in the morning, coming through the window with the cold air.

And with the whirring of the train's frozen axles. Aurora said, Hold your breath! and I blocked my throat as the darkness was pulled over us. The friction of the train on the rails sounded stifled and secret. In the light from the other side of the tunnel, she let her breath leak slowly out between her teeth, her hand slipping the pills into her coat pocket, and I coughed mine out with a gasp. A pair of coattails flapped out of the train compartment after the man who had been sitting next to her. *Vowels*, that's what we called those pills, because they softened you up and made you receptive, starting with a round feeling and a light in your mouth, your throat, your belly and so on, until your whole body was a glowing processor just waiting for data, which was probably why City Church was the perfect market; affiliated with the rehab centre, it was full of addicts who had turned to God or were trying to. The vowels, like the service, lasted for about an hour and were usually a prelude to acid, a way to prepare for the actual trip, so Aurora could get a bag of 100 for £50 and sell them on for £1 apiece. She would prop herself against the wall by the entrance, then push off with her shoulder and greet people as they arrived. She pulled them to her, calling them by name, and leaned into them with her voice. A kind of smoothing, a levelling of features into a dull plate of a face, marked the majority of these people, and from where I was standing it looked like Aurora was pulling them out of their sameness one by one and really seeing them. I thought about whether it felt that way for them too. Whether she could do that while selling them drugs.

What surprised me that day, and what I think Aurora brought me along to see, was how they remained seated when it was all over. From the moment I had taken the pill — in sync with a hundred other hands rising from pocket to mouth, a hundred throats stretching and swallowing when the prelude began — the service had seemed to be elapsing in parallel with my trip, expanding in time with the space being cleared out inside me. As if its composition were encoded into the chemical formula of the pill. Afterwards, there was only the comedown. I was all tied up inside and couldn't feel a thing. And that felt like an awful weakness in light of the service and the way the prayers, the organ music and the priest's gesticulations had filled me up. Now it was quiet, the priest had left, and all around me people remained seated with the saddest faces or their eyes closed, afflicted by something they preferred to deal with in the dark. They sat slumped and shaggy, but seemed at the same time infused with a mystical will to be present in this after, a persistence that went far beyond what the pill could give them. But Aurora! She wouldn't budge either, didn't react to my elbow poking her side or my feet tapping the floor. Of course she sat through the service so people could see that she didn't split as soon as she had milked them, and when the dealer is tripping too you know the product is good. But why was she still sitting there — and with that belly too, shouldn't she eat something soon? Her abdomen was bulging in the light from the barred windows above, trying to get her attention, just like me. She stayed that way for hours. And the church actually wasn't even a church, but a bare room without ornamentation, just concrete walls and ten rows of folding chairs set up for the occasion.

Back home in the kitchen, Rory had a roast in the oven and two homeless men at the table who looked up at us friendly and embarrassed when we walked through the door. Dave and Sully, he said, introducing them with an outstretched palm, we got to talking up by the corner shop. Aurora hid her confusion, probably so that they wouldn't feel unwelcome, went over to greet them with me at her heels and turned to Rory, who had his head in the oven: Food's ready! Over dinner he tried to keep the conversation going, mostly talking about Aurora — only three weeks till she's due but she's still bloody working nine to five — while a tone of accusation crept into his voice. Yeah, things are a bit tight right now, Aurora said, looking at him, especially if we want to be able to afford a roast now and then. She ate very little. And now she's taking Casey with her too, Rory continued. Yeah, I said, I'm not doing much anyway, so I get to go to work with Mum! And I'm here all day thinking about them, Rory said. Well, you've got friends up at the Park, Dave said, implying Sully and himself with an almost noble nod back and forth between them. I smiled, feeling really wretched, sad that they had to step right from the street into this family drama, probably the first home in which they'd set their wiry feet in a while. Rory had insisted they take their socks off and rest their feet on a stool under the table. They were sitting very awkwardly, unable to relax or give in to the reclined position their raised legs demanded. They reeked much worse than we did, everyone could smell them. When Rory offered for them to stay the night, something happened that went way beyond this covert marriage dispute and the discomfort of sitting in the middle of it. Dave, he was the one who did the talking for both of them, looked down and said, Thank you but we can't. But it's freezing cold outside, Rory continued, and the shelters, aren't they all closed now, until Dave said, We wish we could accept the offer. You're very nice people. But you see, it's not easy being comfortable in someone else's home — it can make us really sad, Sully added — we can't do it for your sake.

Later, after we had said goodbye and closed the door behind them, we stood in our respective corners of the kitchen, staring into the living room. It was so full of their honesty and our pent-up conflict that we had two possibilities: either cry or shout at each other, either fight or be sad by ourselves, so we went straight to the bedroom — Rory through the door with Aurora at his heels, me through the hole in the wall — and met in bed in an indecisive embrace. Sex between the three of us could never become that self-contained formation that shut out everything else, the snake biting its own tail, we were always trying to open and extend the pleasure, with hands and mouths, across the mattresses, through the room, up and out of the building. While the train screeched through every ten minutes. Water glasses rattled on the nightstand. The flat bulged red with heat against the night's blue-black. The air was riddled by traffic moving in all directions, up to the satellite and back again. Someone shouted, started running after someone else, Hey, you! Cars accelerated and hit the brakes at the foot of the bed. Aurora's belly was bulbous with visible veins, we navigated around it with caution. At one point I was on my knees with Rory inside me and Aurora lying diagonally in front of me. I was sucking on her nipples and could have sworn some milk came out, just a few drops. Just a second of that body-warm, sugary, a little oniony, a-little-too-soon liquid in my mouth, and right after, an impulse to suck away, to drink so much that it would fill me all the way up and push out Rory's cock, but there wasn't any more. It's not that I didn't appreciate his presence, but there was a longing inside me to be alone with Aurora and be pure milk. Sometimes when he fucked me I could feel so specific and demarcated, bound to the bed. The morning after our first night together he made scrambled eggs and said I should stay around. So strange sitting there together, eating breakfast in a T-shirt on a cold stool, like the two of us were going to be a couple, but then he said, I think Aurora would be happy if you were here when she came home. Rory had a way of being in the flat without her, always in the process of taking care of something or other, which I really liked about him. He would gently rearrange the furniture and clothes, wipe the crumbs off the table, make the bed and air the place out. Water the plants with a spray bottle and nuzzle the leaves between two fingers, count the cash and meticulously decide what kind of soup he would make today, and which ingredients he'd have to steal for it. He dragged everything out, as if to fake a household and make it last until Aurora got in — maybe that was part of why he wanted me to stay? Back then she would come home early, and we would have started flirting around noon, stirring up a mood she could wade right into and release. Later, if he hadn't already that morning, Rory would go do the stealing, and then me and Aurora would make out hungrily and wait to do more until he returned. A lot of me loved her exclusively, wanted her now and all to myself, but 1. that would ruin their marriage; 2. then I might have to leave the flat or at least not be under Rory's care anymore; 3. I cared a lot about Rory too; and 4. it was because of their marriage, with my place in the sweet spot between them, that I could even be close to Aurora in the first place. Without them I might lose her for good.

Now I was looking up and saw a guilty but also kind of outbound expression in her eyes. I looked over my shoulder and realised that they were responding to Rory's, which were looking at her the same way as when we had come home late that afternoon: an injured look that expressed the same feeling that I had had next to her in the City Church all day: she was on her way out. She was turning toward something that made her stay in her seat much longer than necessary, forget to eat and drink, and which made her care about everything but her sales, the baby and us waiting for her at home.

Six months later, I suddenly spot the reflection of the man in the dull grey trench coat in the glass I'm looking out of. In the opposite window, he's sitting with his hands in his lap, letting himself be rocked by the swaying of the train on the tracks. He's staring straight ahead at the empty seat across from him, apparently so familiar with the scenery on this route that he can just as well let it slide blurrily by. Who knows what it's like: being a dealer, spending your days on those efficient, silent transactions. Recognisable, at this point even familiar buyers in the seat across from him, who he can't talk to or really look at, just a second of eye contact to confirm the imminent sale. Maybe it's not only a matter of discretion, maybe he actually prefers it that way, cutting straight to the bone of the transaction: in the dark of the tunnel handing over a ziplock bag with a right hand, taking the cash in a left, getting up and leaving the car before it gets light again. The train turns softly to the left, setting course for an arch of brown bricks that frame a darkness for me. Two deep breaths and I block my throat, haven't been able to breathe in tunnels ever since Aurora told me you couldn't. It's a game she used to play. Hidden by the dark and the mechanical rumbling, I get up and walk over and kneel on the seat behind the dealer. I dip my hands into each of his coat pockets, close them around whatever they're holding, pull them out and walk fast out of the car.

An hour later I'm knocking on Rory and Aurora's door. It hurts in my bones going over there, knowing that I have to see them again, but I really need the money. The sight alone of Rory's puzzled face in the cracked-open door almost makes me cry. He lets me in, and then I'm standing there looking around the kitchen, at the evergreen countertops with all of his lists on them, at the toaster and the kettle, in the yellow glow of the ceiling light. I can feel how my body is sucking everything in because it has forgotten and knows that now's the chance to get it back: the piles of clothes, the draught and the knots in the floor, the smell of Rory's soup, the jagged hole in the wall, Rory, his birdlike body in the kitchen, I swallow it all and hold it inside my wide-open belly. Then I take two steps forward and look into the bedroom to the right. Aurora is sitting on the edge of the bed, rocking a cradle on the floor. Something awkward about the way her arm is extended, she must have sat down like that as soon as she heard it was me. The baby is quiet and barely visible between the hat and blanket, snub nose and a tiny open mouth. What's up? Aurora says. What've you got? I take the bag of vowels out of my pocket and say, There's 98, I took two already. Where'd you get them? she asks. Don't worry about it, I say. You can have £30, she says. You know I know what they cost, I say. I want 40, minimum. You get 30, she says, even more resolved... Listen, I don't want to know where you got those pills, but if our guy has lost 100, and then we buy half the usual amount the next day, how do you think that's going to look? No matter what, I'm gonna have to spread those 98 out over a few weeks, or months... Fine, I say, 30, that's fine.

I handed her the bag of pills. She handed me £30.

I still don't know how we ended up with that cruel transaction. Was it my indecisiveness, my inability to take a stand in the fight, that let the two of them close around each other? Was I just too passive, a kind of pet, was I becoming too dirty and unkempt? Or was it the baby, the arrival of the actual baby, that inevitably excluded me? That would be really ironic, because it was most likely conceived the night we first met. After Dave and Sully left, we lay in bed and counted back to that night, and I felt fertile for a second, or at least beneficial to my surroundings. Me and Rory were curled up on either side of Aurora, who was sitting halfway up in bed, each of us with a cheek and a hand on her belly. You've never been so pregnant, he said dreamily. Soon there'll be a baby here. He gestured panoramically across the room like it was a showroom for their life after the birth.

I realised that the child, or at least the dream of a home that the child was supposed to fulfil, was Rory's most of all. He had never really been good at anything, but the flat was his to arrange, to potter around and display at the end of each day. A helpless living creature here would make him indispensable. The next morning I was awoken by the door slamming, jumped out of bed and caught up with Aurora halfway up the street. Hey, you're pulling my love out of bed way too early! I said, smiling, and grabbed her collar. I didn't think you wanted to come, she said. Her face was blank and exhausted in the headlights of the cars driving by. Sometimes she looked almost wounded by fatigue, it was really cute. I just don't understand what they're doing in that church, I said, why don't they get up at the end? I don't think I can explain that to you, Aurora said, it's a kind of meditation — But I want to be part of it, I said — on the hangover, she said, the state that comes after. Okay, come on then.

The City Church was in East London, Stratford I guess, in a remote industrial neighbourhood twenty minutes walking from Leyton Station, and the patients had already served their five hours when we got there a little before eleven. That was how they paid for their stay at the rehab centre, Aurora told me, by working it off in the factories. The whole complex was owned by one of the private companies that the state had started using to contract its social services. People were sent here after being on benefits for a long time, as a kind of combined detox and job training. Even from a purely therapeutic standpoint, the work played an important role, Aurora explained; getting sober was all about rediscovering your functionality, teaching yourself each day that you're good for something. In the work halls, screens listed the day's productivity figures, and once a month you had to sit in the observation room to watch the *big picture* and be reminded of each person's indispensability on the production line. But *I* always felt totally replaceable, Aurora said. The days I produced the most, it was like it was running right through me. What do they make? I asked. Turbines, computer chips, that kind of thing. A bell rang, or the sound of a bell was played from speakers on the roof of the church, and a few minutes later people left the factories lining the road, and walked down the sidewalk and across the gravel car park. There was something protracted and uncertain about their movements, on the way to yet another demanding job, one they weren't sure they could complete, but also something serene, a kind of faith, maybe, that it was worth doing anyway. On the way into the church, which was actually an empty factory, a box-shaped building with peeling walls and the trunks of demolished chimneys sticking out of the roof, they stopped by Aurora to exchange £1 for a vowel with a handshake or an embrace across her belly. She was pale and professional in the late morning sun.

Inside, we sat on folding chairs, swallowed our pills and listened to the prelude. After a few minutes I felt the light of the vowel expanding my body, activating an alternative nervous system that was directly connected to everything around me. My skull and my rib cage enveloped the hall, the organ and the sermon quivered inside me. As the priest pronounced the blessing he melted into my spine with a fluid click, pushing my ribs from each other with his arms. Our addiction was a hallmark, the sign of a foundational weakness and impotence that we had to accept in order to let God accomplish inside us that which we couldn't do ourselves. And when we speak of God, we mean God as you perceive him. He said that several times.

There's nothing to say about the séance after the service. No altar, no ornaments in the empty, square room could distract me from the unbearable feeling of paralysis or permanent sedation of my soul with which I was left after the trip. Even the light was useless, falling without shadows or nuances, it probably hadn't been changed since there was a factory here. After a few hours I started getting hungry, and what about Aurora, could she feel the baby complaining inside her? Was she ignoring it like she was able to ignore her own hunger? The air was greasy from the gas that had been burned in the room. Grease got stuck in my eyes and the roots of my nails, and I felt the creeping griminess I remembered from living on the street, before I moved in with Rory and Aurora, in an inhuman crowd of people and vehicles. It's a boundless space, not fit for living, you can't tidy or clean or decorate anything. You own nothing around you.

When the bell finally rang again, who knows when, we got up in a daze from our folding chairs and left the church in the opposite direction of everyone else. They squeezed past us, heading toward the back wall. On the threshold I turned around, grabbed Aurora's hand and watched them disappear through a double door made of dark-green metal. They stepped out onto a muddy field, in the dusk that fell murkily into the church. What are they doing? I asked. The rehab centre, Aurora said, it's on the other side of the field, and pulled my arm. I hesitated for a second, trying to make out a building, but saw only blue-grey fog framed by the doorway, and the patients sliding away, disappearing into it, one by one, in the middle of the field.

Several worn faces looked up at us as if we had interrupted them in the middle of a sentence or a prayer. At least ten homeless men and women were seated around the table, on the two barstools in the kitchen, on the floor against the opposite wall and on the windowsill, with their bare feet resting on stools and piles of clothes, in a stench that made the flat swell. It was completely silent for maybe five seconds, until a bony woman with long, iron-grey hair burst out laughing from the window and said, They weren't expecting that, were they now! Just look at those two! Rory laughed too, goofily resting his hands on our necks. But they're totally speechless, the woman said, haven't they seen a homeless person before? And in their nice little living room too. Come on, give them a break, Ellen, said a slightly younger man at the kitchen table, let them get through the door, all right? And I'm not doing that, or what, Ellen said, not giving them a chance? No, you're not, the man said. I'm just teasing them a bit, she said, just joking around. I mean, they look like they're at the zoo! And that's no problem *at all*. That's just *fine*. We are a bunch of old seals, the two of us and the others, a flock of crows, free birds in a cage that's too big? No, we're not, there was a third who said, we're wild dogs, and then their eyes and voices kind of let go of us and turned to each other, so we could throw off our jackets and turn to Rory, who was awkwardly stirring his soup. His cheekbones shone boyishly in the steam. Up in front of the shelter, he said quietly, I stopped by on the way home from the shop. And they were all standing there freezing and their numbers weren't getting called, you know, it's completely packed tonight. There's a storm coming. So I said they should come over here to warm up and have a bite to eat... You know, honey, I want us to be able to take care of people here, just provide the bare necessities. That's why we have a home, right? Someday you'll be old too! Ellen shouted over everyone else. She had gotten up from the windowsill and was hanging in the middle of the room, her crinkled skin aglow like a paper lamp, like an ancient creature on speed. Ellen, Rory said, and went to meet her on the floor. Calmly, he placed his hands on her shoulders and looked her in the eye, as sure of himself as he was when he stole. Do you think they understand the insanity of being sixty years old? she shouted. I don't think they do, Rory said. They're not listening to me, she said, they all think they'll just die in their sleep whenever they're ready. But you know a thing or two, Rory said, that's for sure. Yeah, just look at me, Ellen said. Here I am, spent my whole life on the street, getting ready to die, and still I'm afraid! Still, I want my life. I can't take it anymore, not for another second. Don't think about that right now, Rory said, it's time to eat. I made pea soup. She thought about it for a second. Yeah, she said, sinking into herself, I'm so hungry.

The rest of the night he took care of everyone, ladling and clearing the table, moving things around and making soft encampments out of pillows and clothes, with a new spring in his step. And at the same time he was trying too hard, wriggling his hips, carrying four bowls of soup with demonstrative ease whenever Aurora was watching, as if to say, Look! You too could be this nimble and caring if you hadn't spent all day wearing yourself out in the pews. I leaned toward her, attempting to squeeze myself into the place he was trying to appeal to. I avoided making conversation with the homeless people. In the corner of my eye, they were a wall of voices, a greyish fog, and I felt ashamed. But I couldn't see anything in them but fatigue. That deep, undying fatigue that takes over a face and settles inside it. Too much bad weather and bad sleep, too much noise, abuse and traffic, that was all they expressed. That was what spooked me about them, the way their features had yielded to a far-too-general and shared condition. It hadn't happened to me, not in the year and a half I was living on the street, which was part of why I was able to find a clean set of clothes, dress up, go to the bar and flirt my way home with Rory and Aurora. Now they were saying good night, and I hurried after them into the bedroom. We got into bed and listened to the storm and the snores of the homeless people. One of them had put their feet through the hole in the wall. I had the urge to chop them off at the ankles.

On the train the next day, both Aurora and the trees on the other side of the glass, which I loved, and in which the sun slowly rose, were dead to me. In the church, when the high started to fade, I recognised the down as the same condition of insufficiency: not being able to give the world back the meaning I knew it had, for me too. For hours I sat there, feeling that absence, and it hurt in my bones like they were crumbling.

Aurora shouted hi and walked straight to the bedroom in long leaping strides to avoid stepping on anyone. They were everywhere and more since yesterday, strewn across the floor, talking and tea-drinking, slumped over like the participants in a shabby symposium. I was on the toilet, my buttocks freezing, when her voice cut hostile through the wall, quickly followed by Rory's. Without being finished I pulled up my trousers, ran across the living room and stopped at the door to the bedroom. Do you have any sense, Aurora was shouting, do you have any idea what it's like? If you're so fucking pregnant, Rory said, why don't you come home and relax when you're done working? Why are you staying out so late? But you've got a room full of people! she said. Yeah! I said, and took a long step into the room, maybe you should be taking a little more care of *them*. I nodded in the direction of Aurora's belly. This all started long before I started helping those people, Rory said, and don't you try to teach me anything! You're the one out with her all day, what the fuck are you thinking? I'm taking care of her, I said, and looked at Aurora. As she stood there on the bed, emaciated and bulging like a chicken carcass picked clean, with one hand under her belly and the other raised at Rory, I realised that I had completely forgotten about her in the church the last few days. I felt the kind of sadness that collapses in your belly when you realise the person you love and live with is lonely. In the hallway, some of the homeless people were pulling on their boots. Rory ran over and blocked the door with outstretched arms. But you're already here! he said. We don't want to intrude, they said. It's just a little squabble, he said, lowering his voice, the

kind of thing that happens when you live together. My wife...
it really doesn't have anything to do with you. Stay, won't you?
He came back in, got up close to Aurora and hissed into her
ear: Come back home to me when you've done your thing. The
violent potential in his voice reminded me of that night when
the pot of soup was steaming away in her absence. All of a
sudden, he got up and hurled it at the wall and made the hole
through which the homeless people's awkward silence was
now audible. There was soup everywhere. Then you get rid
of all these people, Aurora said. If you don't come home late
again, he said.

That night, I was awoken by the sound of scratching. It
lasted for five seconds at a time, accompanied by a sharp and
dry vibration in my spine, like someone was running a bar-
ber's knife slowly down it. I lay there, getting scared, heard
someone breathing between the scratching, counted to three
and rolled fast onto my stomach. Between two of the pallet
planks I could make out the bottom of a face, a small, tight
mouth without lips, which opened and said sorry. What the
hell are you doing! I said. You can't sleep there, you really
can't. But it's just me, she said – Ellen, I said – I like it here, it's
better than the living room. Her breath was sweet and dry. We
debated a bit. She sounded harmless and frail in the dark, and
I couldn't be tough. Okay, I said, and turned onto my back, but
can you at least stop scratching? I'll try, she said, and started
up again a while later. And then I couldn't help but imagine
that we were buried together like a married couple, Ellen below, tirelessly scratching the lid of her coffin. It's like that for
some people, I think it is, maybe for most; they have to lie in

the ground and practice dying because they didn't manage to get ready while they were alive. Their whole existence reduced to a dry breath in ash, a leg stretching, the sound of nails on wet wood.

The next day I couldn't even enjoy the service. The high, the way the vowel turned me into one big glowing nervous system, felt mostly like an opportunity or a demand I couldn't live up to. The hunger and numbness that would follow shone dull and desertlike through the euphoria, and drove it away. I had the thought that this feeling would never stop, and couldn't shake it off. It made my intestines contract, and then I felt a jab, like from a little piece of cold iron, deep in my belly. Some of me passed through the hole in a quick and piercing movement, as if it were being snatched up by a bird of prey, into some foggy, directionless landscape, but it didn't make me less sad.

I still don't understand, I said when we were sitting on the train headed back home. Aurora turned her face from the glass and looked at me. She was actually ugly, or at least each individual feature was unattractive — snub nose, narrow pursed lips, dull eyes set deep in her face — but she was beautiful. I don't understand why you take those pills... why you hang around after. Oh, Casey, she said, exhausted, you've been there too. How would you explain it? Terrible, I said, I just feel weak. Me too, said Aurora... but that feeling, it's like it's right for me. I think it's what I am. Are you scared? I asked. Of what? The baby, I said. Why, it's coming either way. But you can still be scared. Ahead, the dark semicircle of the Thames tunnel approached behind her. It rose and gradually filled more and more of the grey sky, and as we entered it she said, I'm just tired, Case. I'm so tired of waking up every morning at the crack of dawn with this light in my body. I wake up with such a dumb, totally physical *appetite for the day* when I should stay in bed. And with a baby in my belly when I don't feel like it... like it should be there. There shouldn't be anything there. It makes me so hateful.

The train raced through the tunnel, both jangling over the tracks and drifting away, the darkness expanding the space. The exit signs swished by, gave way to Aurora's face. I reached a hand across the table and placed it on her wet hands. But I'm not scared, she said. I couldn't come up with anything else to say besides that I was there for her and would play with the baby and give it milk at night when she didn't have the energy, and then I could see it: me and the kids, there were two of them now, wrapped in our blankets in front of the television before Rory and Aurora got up. Rory had built a loft in the living room.

The flat was aired out and the makeshift beds cleared away, but it was full of people whom he must have picked up as soon as he realised we weren't coming back early after all. There was something pointless and impotent about his protest now that he had said it out loud. Like stirring a pot full of water. We woke up around midnight to a fresh wet mattress. Aurora pushed us away, panting through her contractions alone. The light from the cars slid bluish across her forehead and hair. Two of the homeless people came in to ask whether she was okay. I hurried to push them back into the living room, where the others were sitting up in their beds, not knowing what to do with themselves. I started tucking them in, pulling the blankets up to their chins, placing a hand on their foreheads, but stopped when Aurora came out of the room, and ran to grab her hospital bag instead. In the middle of the room, she hesitated and said to Rory that she refused to give birth until they were all out of the flat. He turned to them, clapped three times and asked them to leave. Get them out of here! Aurora screamed. They hastily threw on all of their layers, laced up their boots and walked past her with their eyes on the ground. Let's get going, Rory said. Her too, Aurora said... Casey too, she repeated without looking up, but sent an exhausted nod in my direction. Get her out! Rory turned toward me, and he was about to get it past his lips when I handed him the bag and left, on legs that felt ancient and foreign, through the door, down the stairs and out onto the street.

I took the train to Stratford and walked straight through the empty church. In front of me, still framed by the wide-open iron door, the field and the overcast night sky slid into a big pile of mud. It thawed and received me to the ankles. There wasn't a single light or star, only the cold, wet wind I imagined was coming from the sea to the east. What was there for me in the east? I walked back and forth, all around, in and out of the mud that was warmer and sweeter than the air. My eyes adjusted to the darkness, but then came the fog. I lay down on my stomach and fell asleep. At some point, I was awakened by some sticky sounds, and out of the damp, white fog there came two, then ten, then twenty and then a whole crowd, muddy and tired like me. I slid in between them and walked alongside them. When we reached the industrial quarter by the City Church, I followed them into a random hall and stamped computer chips for hours. After the service, I followed them back across the field, found a bed that was free in a room for five and was inaugurated into Group Therapy: taking turns, you talked for fifteen minutes about whatever you were feeling, while the others listened without judgment and helped you get to the Hurt, the places where the pain lay hidden. Reaching them would cause bodily reactions: sweats, shakes, farts, tears, yawns and laughter. I slept and ate and showered, serving my five hours at a new factory each day. Everywhere the buzzing of machines, and the fixed direction of the production line that I started to follow from hall to hall. In the factories closest to the church, work was easy and manual. We welded computer chips, cast rotor blades and fans, put together plastic and electronic parts, carrying out a few motions in a process that resulted in a processor, turbine, or motherboard. Farther out they were assembled into respirators, and in an adjacent hall, into servers that were transported to a building about the size of two football pitches and full of server racks in dead-straight rows. A set of keys and a laptop were pushed toward me through a crack in the wall, and for the next five hours, I followed the others: strolled up and down the rows, connected the computer to the servers that lit up red and followed the troubleshooting instructions on the screen until they stopped. Meanwhile, I saw glimmers of what was stored on them: data about individual patients, their productivity figures, medical files, records, transcripts of Group Therapy. Much of it was quantified, entered into charts I couldn't interpret. That I could move freely between the halls also meant I didn't have to work, I knew that. But I wanted to see where the respirators ended, and the hours of repetition made my grief foggy and mechanical, my feeling of not meaning anything to anyone. I missed Aurora all the time. One morning, in the parking lot in front of the church, someone recognised me and asked where she was. She needed to take care of some things, I said, as people flocked around me. She told me to tell you guys to go on without her. The last part just slipped out, but they looked like they understood. And without the vowels, one of them said. We need to continue authenticating our addiction. Some days, when crossing the field, a bird of prey would emerge from the clouds, and we would lean our heads back, watching it dive with its long, stiff neck and its claws. At the rehab centre, we had the afternoons off and could relax in the rec room where the lighting was low and ambient. It made you want to sit on the rug or in one of the furnished corners and chat with the other patients, or with the nurses moseying about at our disposal. There was always somcone to talk to. And I discovered a pressing need to talk, a whole database of thoughts, feelings, fantasies and memories and quiverings in my nerves, that suddenly became accessible to me. Things felt true when I said them aloud. One day, with the help of a stolen ID, I entered the fenced enclosure farthest from the church, wearing a lab coat like the other employees I had seen coming out of there. The tall brick building was full to the rafters with a cool, rattling sound like wind in fallen leaves. Separated by stands bearing respirator equipment, hospital beds were arranged side by side in long rows, sixty or eighty beds total, housing the Newly Dead: warm, breathing, urinating and pulsating corpses that blood was being drawn from and drugs were being tested on, until it was time to harvest their organs. I was careful not to bump into their bare feet, their fresh faces. I recognised some of them from the centre: people who had committed suicide or overdosed, I had seen the nurses rushing to their rooms with the defibrillator.

Bad Mexican Dog

The sky is overcast through and through, the beach still covered in silent bodies. There's a sweet, heavy, electric smell of thunder and sweat. There's a time, between when the rain appears in the clouds and when it hits their bodies, that the guests refuse to believe it. They're still lying there, in 24 rows of 20, with glossy tanned stomachs and sunglasses on because they've paid to lie in the sun. The drops fall and prick the sand dark, shattered by the plastic of the beach chairs, multiplying, impossible to tell apart from the sea and the sky and the beach. The guests cling to the shafts of their parasols, but the white fabric is quickly soaked and dripping. 'Parasols look ridiculous without the sun,' Jia says, laughing. 'They're completely beside themselves.' The guests look in our direction for help, but when it's raining we're supposed to leave them to themselves. It's something the owner came up with, to remind

117

them of the exclusive order they're paying for. And the benefit of getting themselves a personal boy: only Manu is still on the sand. He's carrying the French lady's bag, shielding her with a tarp he found in the storage room when he smelled the rain this morning. Stooped, they weave through rows of beach chairs, turn onto the boardwalk and pass the bamboo bar and reception hut. A corner of the French-Spanish dictionary she uses for their lessons is poking out of her bag, getting wet; the pages are swelling. His hair sticks to his back between his shoulder blades. Up on the boulevard, he helps her into the back seat of a cab and is about to shut the door when a long, bony arm reaches out and pulls him inside.

When the cab is gone I turn my head and look at the beach like the others: Jia, Ginger and the new boy, Bill, with his thin, combed-back hair and, when he doesn't know you're looking, a slightly wounded expression on his square face. We stand in a row beneath the reception's palm-frond roof, in the steam that won't leave our bodies in the saturated air. Behind us stands the owner, smoking. The surface of the ocean is dissolved in grimy grey fog without a horizon. The beach is becoming part of the sky too; streams of rain and dirt from the boulevard turn the sand liquid. Beach chairs are pulled out of file, look like insects floating around in an ancient tequila sunrise, shades of red at the bottom: beach boy blood and the blood we shed to get them back. The rain stirs it up like it makes the rocks give off the earthy smell of *their* blood, like it makes the living water in the changing room overflow: between the guests, little sandy slime creatures rise for a moment and groan before they're swept away by the current and dissolve. The rain makes the best of what it's got. Its smell makes us calm, I can hear it in our breath filling the air beneath the awning. 'All right, boys,' the owner says, tossing the smoking cigarette butt over our heads. 'The rain is winding down. When it's gone I want everything back in order.'

There's supposed to be 480 beach chairs total, 24 perfect rows of 20, and we're 4 boys, it's a demanding job. First, we comb the sand with a broad-toothed rake until it's Bounty-white again. Seaweed and tubes of lotion, magazines, plastic packaging and bottles mount into piles that we load into the dumpster behind the changing room, at the back of the square bamboo hut. And then Jia sets up the tool we use to restore order after rain: a pole five yards tall with a clear, pyramid-shaped crystal on top that refracts the sunlight in a grid of orange rays. From the crystal's square bottom they're projected all across the beach. At the zenith, the grid is perfect: we run up and down our rows, placing a chair at each point. Halfway through, I feel nausea on an empty stomach and acid in my legs, but if the setup takes more than ten minutes, it starts to strike the eye. Just a bit of quivering is fine, the owner says, a weak vibration along the rows, that's how you introduce time into the grid.

While I'm on all fours trying to catch my breath, someone places a hand on my neck and runs their fingers through my hair. I look up at Manu, who's broad and dark with the sun behind him.

'Where've you been?' I ask.

'Working.' He smiles, holding a fist full of cash down in front of me.

'We could have used your hands down here,' I say.

'Oh, c'mon,' he says. 'You know I would never touch that old hag. And actually, that's not what she wants either—'

'That's not what I meant.'

'She wants a... grandchild. A young, little friend she can cultivate and converse with. People her own age are so boring, she says, they don't have any passions anymore.' He leans over, tightening his grasp on my neck when he moves his lips to my ear. His breath is the same temperature as the air, but drier. He says, 'You know you're the only one I want to touch,' and there's tenderness and also something aggressive or threatening in his voice. Ever since he started seeing the French lady with the sun hat, something harsh has come over him, a big, stony parasol, forcing its shadow through his face and limbs. He carries himself more with his shoulders than his hips now. He speaks to me and touches me like he's trying to get closer and farther away from me at the same time. It makes me sad. It turns me on. He pushes my head into the sand and runs away laughing. I jump up and sprint after him, grab him from behind, and we tumble into the sea.

Then it's night and he pushes me headfirst into the pool in front of the bench in the changing room. Seawater steams orange, comes up to the middle of my thighs. It's thick and living with the jellyfishy blobs we've been filling it up with day after day; they've fused with each other and the salt:

little, veined whitish eggs bulging in clusters. I'm on all fours in front of Manu, who's on his knees, feeding me the living water, shovelling it into my ass with his hand. The sun is inside me now because the sun sets in the ocean. Then he shows me a transparent, hollow shrimp shell he found on the beach, sticks his hand into his swim trunks and pulls out his long, thin dick. 'Do you want to?' he asks, nodding, and I nod too, and he twists the head off the shell and softens the rest in the living water. It fits snug around his dick except for the legs dangling from its base. I let myself float in the pool with my back arched and my ass in the air, let myself relax inside and feel him slide in: a ribbed and prickling sensation in the slime and cold. Through the hole in the wall, the sun makes a column of light in the water. He moves inside me, my spine turns to jelly. I can feel the eggs inside it: we're throbbing at the base of the spine, wandering slowly through the abdomen. Squirt of thick white juice, first Manu inside me and then me with eggs in the sun lands on the sandy ground. We make the best of what we've got. Through the slimy membrane I can see the other eggs hatching, and out of the bubbles a few elongated creatures swim clumsily away, laughing, intertwined with each other, rolling around in the stirred-up sand. Something hits my face, a soft foot in my belly. I hit the ground and am thrown back toward the other small bodies in the light. In a glimpse, a glowing red eye is laughing at me through the membrane. A thin leg across my upper body holds me down while someone tickles my belly with their antennae. I laugh and wriggle against the membrane, flapping and kicking with all of my legs. And then suddenly I hatch and start moving.

Arched along my ass, my limbs like organic paddles, I move through the water, gliding, steady, at a speed that feels just right for my little body. The other boys are somewhere in the water too. We are all very small.

We were on our way out to get breakfast when the receptionist with the narrow, tired eyes, who had given us recommendations for restaurants and things to do in Cancún, and let us know at least once a day that he was at our service, came running after us with an envelope. Lasse's face stiffened when it was placed in his hands, and he asked who it was from. 'Don't know,' the receptionist said, 'it was on the counter when I got in this morning.' But what about the security cameras, Lasse asked, they must have gotten it on tape? The receptionist shook his head, no cameras, and was already on his way back down the sea-blue carpet that led to the reception desk. 'No cameras!?' I said, hadn't thought of that before, but now I felt unsafe and angry that there wasn't some form of surveillance, 'so anyone can just barge in here with gross white envelopes, without being caught on tape?' and there weren't any guards either, anyone could just walk in here and start shooting. Lasse fished a DVD and a typewritten letter out of the envelope. If we wanted to stop the video from being posted online, we would have to drop a fairly large amount of cash in a mailbox at the specified address before midnight, and going to the police would cost us more than money. Remember this is Mexico, the last line read.

It's just like in the movies, I thought, but not for long, because when we were watching the video in bed on Lasse's computer it was like it contained a clone of me. I felt the boy's warm dry mouth when he licked my foot on screen, and the electric shudder his tongue sent up my body from my toes. The shaking voice abusing him in my throat. I felt it exactly in time with it happening on screen, which convinced me that the woman in there was a living, sentient creature who was somehow connected to me. The video was paused, and Melanie's hoarse voice was in my ear: 'You should have never followed him to that hotel, that's rule number one: Never let yourself be isolated. You should be glad you weren't mugged.' I felt her sarong against my leg and realised that she was sitting next to me in bed. 'It's not that bad, is it?' Lasse asked on my other side, placing a hand on my shoulder. 'Won't people be able to tell that we were tricked into doing this?' He played the video again, and I couldn't tell how we would come across, could only feel that I was living a life of my own in there, which made me afraid that that would also be the case in the mind of anyone else watching, whether they knew me or not.

'We're paying the money,' I said.

'But honey, they want 30,000 pesos,' Lasse said.

'I don't want this video getting out,' I said.

While we were taking out cash, Melanie went to the bike rental place to ask Mateo, her local flirtation, whether we could borrow his car. The drop-off spot was a bit inland, ten or fifteen miles west of town, on a secluded street in the light-green landscape of my GPS. Sighing, stubborn, unnecessarily slow, Lasse entered the PIN code to our shared bank account, which we had to use to make the full amount.

He felt screwed over, I knew, after having spent weeks planning our trip to be as cheap as possible. Maybe that's why he asked Mateo, who had insisted on coming with us, to stop at a roadside café in the old city. It was one of those places — dirty, almost empty, with white plastic chairs and menus in Spanish — that always appealed to Lasse: not because of its possible authenticity, but because the food was probably cheap. I'd never understood his stinginess, at least not when it came to money. He made a good enough salary as a high school teacher, and his parents gave him money whenever he needed it. It was more like he was walking around inside a computer game that he could win if he came back from the other side of the globe having actually saved money. No one could think for a second that they would get money out of him.

And then he ordered the most expensive dish on the menu anyway, with extra coffee and freshly squeezed orange juice. I wasn't hungry, but I should eat something, Melanie said, I was pale, and bought me a plate of huevos rancheros. The salsa jump-started my system, making me sweat through the shell that enclosed me. The air was cool beneath the awning and full of dust from the road that sloped down to the porch, the cars rushed past at eye level. I kicked off my flip-flops and rested my feet on the tile floor. It was sticky and smelled like synthetic citrus. Melanie lit a cigarette and looked at me like she was examining me.

'What?' I said when her gaze started to feel greasy on my neck.

'There's no reason to be afraid, darling,' she said, and a second later, when I didn't respond: 'I know, it's not nice to see yourself on tape like that... but now it's just about money. Nothing else is going to happen.'

'Yeah, is there even anything to worry about?' Lasse asked,

looking at Mateo. 'I mean, he's just a boy. What's he going to do if we don't pay?'

'Post it on the internet,' I said.

'You don't know who he's working for,' Mateo said. 'I doubt he's on his own.'

'But isn't this supposed to be one of the safer parts of Mexico?' Lasse asked.

'Yes, the cartels have other things to take care of, I'm sure.' Mateo couldn't help laughing, but stopped when he met Lasse's eyes. 'If that's what you're thinking... It could be anyone, though, people who need the money. And hey, sorry to tell you, but you're pretty much on your own here.'

'You don't say,' I snorted.

'Think of it as protection money,' Melanie said, 'a kind of tax you pay to be safe. Just like back home. Except here it's not the state you're paying... And you can afford it, right?'

'That tax is almost as much as the whole trip,' Lasse said, looking down at his plate, angry and a bit ashamed. He hated when people asked about his personal finances.

Am I scared? I thought, as we left the city, driving past supermarkets, garages, concrete apartment blocks, ranches behind stone walls and wrought-iron gates — is it fear I'm feeling? The boy appeared before me, on all fours on the balcony, on the beach with his school papers in his bag, and I realised that all of my feelings were directed at him, at him and at Lasse who was clucking behind the camera as it captured me. Not at some shadowless boss who might/might not come after us if we didn't give them the money, that didn't mean a thing to me right now. The sky was getting darker. The palm and plantain trees along the road looked more evergreen, less tropical, in cloudy weather. 'Now it's raining,' I said, nodding toward the back window. Over Cancún, the sky contracted into a grey-black mushroom with a whitish stalk of rain. 'Only on the tourists,' Mateo said, and he was right: the clouds seemed to be moving across Isla Cancún, the long sandy isthmus that the resort was built on. The old city was sort of sheltered by the skyline of hotels and the lagoon. Lasse was drawing circles on my shoulder with his finger. The soft dip of the power lines between telephone poles calmed me. Mateo followed the GPS instructions and turned down a narrow road paved with pale, grainy asphalt, a stone wall on our right and a few low wooden houses on our left. 'I've never been here,' he said. A sharp, electric jab shot through my thighs and again I recalled the sensation of my foot in the boy's mouth; for me that was all there was: his tongue touching the skin under my big toe, the touch that bound us against my will, and which repeated in the electric quivering in my nerves and the computer's circuit every time the video played. For a moment, it seemed irrelevant whether the film came out or not. In a sense, the bodies and movements inside it would exist whether or not it was watched, slumbering in the CD drive of Lasse's computer.

The asphalt stopped and turned into gravel. The pale-green overgrowth grew denser and higher, completely obstructing our vision. After a few more miles, here and there a little garbage or scraps of metal in the ditch on the side of the road, Mateo stopped at a yellowed white mailbox mounted on a wooden pole between the trees lining the road. 'Here,' he said, glancing in the rearview mirror. 'You better hurry.' Lasse got out and walked over to the mailbox, lifted the lid and looked inside. Then he straightened up and squinted into the forest, and I recognised the aggression in his body: his limbs tensed, his jaw and lips twitching, like he was about to shout at the trees, the bushes and the grass, 'Well, we're here! Come and get your money!' 'Just do it, babe,' I yelled out the window in Danish. He looked at me through the front window and threw the envelope into the mailbox. On his way back to the car, he kicked a tree at the edge of the ditch, a half-stripped tree about as thick as his own leg, and kept kicking, relentlessly, his arms swinging at his sides, adding a little extra force, maybe seven or ten times until finally the trunk split and he stopped to catch his breath.

When we're done getting dressed, shrimp shell on Manu's dick in my spine soft jelly with eggs in the sun on the sandy ground, we spend all our money on bread and cheese and orange juice and head over to Jia and Ginger's. They live on the outskirts of the old city behind the lagoon. Their narrow room is cool and wet in a stone building with cracked tile floors and peeling walls, but cosy and warm when we're all there. We walk through the door and throw ourselves on the double mattress to the left, except Bill, who stands in the middle of the room, surveying his boring surroundings: in the opposite corner there's a set of hot plates, a sink and a toaster, and on the one wall a shelf with a radio that he turns on. 'Let me make those grilled cheeses,' he says after a while, and walks stiffly to the kitchen. When ten minutes later he serves up a heap of grilled cheese sandwiches, sliced and swollen and shining with fat, Jia looks up at him and says, 'Bill! That's one gorgeous mountain of cheese!' 'There's egg in there too,' Bill says, smiling down at the floor. 'Come here, you old boy,' Jia says, grabbing his knees so he falls on top of us, and we tickle and nip him gently, rolling around in bed with an old, stiff-legged man — a little afraid that his frail limbs might break, until the warm and the jelly begin to spread through them. He laughs and spreads a little into us.

So we eat and drink on our bellies in bed, the juice very cold in my throat. Manu pulls the melted cheese out of his sandwich in a long string that he winds around his fingers, making different animals that we have to bite if we want to be them. His hands are supple and salty. Afterward we play the game where we impersonate guests from the club: the Canadian businessman, the Italian women with the golden fans, the Burn Victim, the Mermaid, Bloody Gary. We imitate their body types and their gaits, the way they sunbathe and wave us over, and when someone guesses right, it's time for the telepathy round. Then you have to choose someone who's supposed to read in your mind what you want to do to the guests. Rip out their insides and use them to tie a bunch of beach chairs into a raft, pour acid into their after-sun, things like that mostly. But you never know for sure who is thinking what. It's pulled out of your body and planted inside it at the same time, just like at the beach club, except that here we're together and cheering and laughing whenever something sounds funny. Ginger is tuning through empty frequencies on the radio, making a soundtrack for the telepathy. A man with a full beard and dead-tired watery eyes pokes his head in to ask if we can quiet down. And we should really open a window, you can't see your own hand in front of you. The voices of two excited kids reach us through the door, and a woman trying to calm them down. A bit farther away, a television and a crowd of mumbling male voices. Fatigue buzzes in all my joints and pulls me to the throbbing ground, deep beneath the building. Manu puts a frying pan on his head and pulls on his skin so it hangs like curtains off his bones. 'The French lady with the sun hat!' I yell, and I'm right, and he picks me for the telepathy round.

I stand in front of him on the cool tiles. The air between our bare bellies is full and bulging with our warmth. Manu's hair clings to his temples and cheekbones and frames his eyes: dark and sad and a little afraid but also radiating a hardness that holds me back. A glittering shrug of stone, sun and sand spreads a mile-long resort across the elongated island behind the lagoon. At one of the hotels, a room on the eighth floor lights up in the light-blue night. The French lady, in an unbuttoned silk shirt with the duvet on her lap, is reading in bed with pills and wine on the nightstand. Manu comes out of the bathroom with a towel wrapped around his waist and walks toward her. 'What's in his head?' Bill asks, whooping. 'What is he going to do to her?' 'He... he's going to lay next to her in bed,' I say, and I see it: the French lady putting down her book, lifting the duvet, giving Manu a determined smile. Something despairing runs into his eyes along with a little water. He shakes his head. 'Nooo,' says Ginger, 'it's not like that!' Manu curls up in her arms, with his hands folded in his lap and his face in the mattress. 'Yeah, but no, it's because he wants to...'

I try to come up with something, that's how the game works, the other person is the only one who knows what's true, as I see her take his hand and make it caress her hip. 'He wants to fill her bed with jellyfish!' I say. 'That's why he's snuck into her room!' Manu nods and tries to regain control of his face, but the water is spilling over his eyes. The others can't see from the mattress, and laugh. 'So when she gets into bed,' I say, 'then all the jellyfish will sting her with their poison through the sheets, that's where he put them, inside the mattress — so she'll be numb... and then the crabs will have free rein.' 'The crabs?' asks Bill. 'Yeah, the carnivorous crabs under the bed,' Manu confirms, and turns his scalp to me while the other boys shout with joy on the mattress.

The next day I'm a personal boy for an American business-man who tells me that life is full of opportunities, your brain is full of products, most people think thoughts every day that could make them rich, but don't dare to pull them out of their foreheads. 'Let's say you're out fishing, for example. You're walking down a trail through the woods, that stretch you have to walk, from the parking lot to the edge of the lake. Insects are flapping, birds are singing, a dragonfly hangs for a mo-ment in the sun between the trees, and you're struggling with your fishing rod as usual. It's too long to carry horizontally across the path, it'll get caught in the branches if you put it in your backpack, it won't balance in your hand, and regardless there'll be a tangle of straw and leaves and dirt and shit in the line. Why the hell don't I have a holster for my fishing rod? you ask yourself. Why don't I have a fucking bag?'

The man is getting red in the face from the sun and his talking, and he looks at me like I should be too. He lifts his head off the beach chair so his neck gets veiny and swells. I lather him up and look like I'm listening, the whole time aware of Manu sluggishly sauntering between beach chairs three rows over. This morning he stepped out of a cab wearing sunglasses, a shirt and sandy-white trousers that showed off his ankles.

'So that's when you've got two options,' the American continues. 'Either you keep asking yourself that same question or you give the world an answer. And then you invent that case. What do you think I did?'

'You invented that case.'

'Yes, impact-resistant, with a horizontal closure and all!' I can't see Manu anymore, he's disappeared between the beach chairs that shimmer and quiver and capture everything in their grid: the guests' glistening skin, the parasols, our lethargic steps across the sand, the sun's steps across the sky. The sun is a service we offer the guests.

'Think about a kid like you,' the American says. 'You must get tons of good ideas running around here all day.'

'Well, yeah,' I say, and see my chance to score a good tip. 'Maybe some shoes or lotion to get rid of the pain in my feet.' Most people will give you a little extra if they feel bad for you, and even more if they feel a bit guilty. But you can't just tell it like it is, out of the blue, *my body hurts*, it'll cramp their mood. 'Sometimes I think about how far I'd get, if I walked the miles I walk in a day, in a straight line down the beach.'

But this guy is untouchable, all business, he says, 'That's a fine thought, but you're not gonna sell that to anyone but yourself. You need to look at the big picture. Can you do my back?'

Meanwhile, he keeps talking, about market segmentation and behavioural economics and the small computer he recently built into the case so you can upload your catch *on location*, and his excited voice makes me rub the sunscreen in way too fast, which gives him that piece-of-meat feeling, and they don't like that, so I get a bad tip.

In the middle of the next back, which I remember to lather slowly and deeply, massaging like I want to get to know all its knots, I see Manu step out of the changing room and over to the bar. He tightens his watch in an arrogant way, outstretched wrist and face turned to the ground out of contempt for the sun. The clothes don't fit him right. He grants the beach a quick glance and starts in a slightly hurried stride up the boardwalk. At its end, the French lady in the sun hat is waiting by a cab, accompanied by the owner of the club. I drop the bottle of lotion and start running through the grid, weaving between guests and boys, as Manu gets into the back seat. The owner and the French lady exchange a handshake, and he closes the door after her. As the cab swings out and slides into the stream of cars on the boulevard, I bolt past the owner on the boardwalk. I run down the sidewalk with my eyes fixed on the pink vehicle disappearing and reappearing between the other cars, almost fifty yards ahead and gone. Then Manu's hand appears in the back window, pressed against the glass, his fingers stretched slightly apart. I run after his hand as everything around me blurs and flickers. The sound of traffic gets more and more distant until I can hear the blood pulsating in my temples in time with his hand swelling. The road slopes and snakes into a two-lane mountain road: dry brown walls of earth on both sides, brownish overgrowth speckled green, pale and yellow, bare rock here and there. In the middle of it all, Manu's colossal, furrowed palm retreating up the mountain, simultaneously luring me in and refusing me entry. I want to give it a kiss. And then it disappears around a rock face, and I collapse on the side of the road and throw up.

A cool, earthy smell of something wet gets me back on my feet and pulls me down along the ledge between bushes and low trees. Their crowns interweave in a dense foliage. Underneath, it's dark with glowing speckles of compacted light. Feeling returns to my feet, which throb and sting where the skin has been worn off, not used to asphalt. My throat is swollen and dry, I can taste vomit on the back of my tongue. I want to lie down on the cold ground, curl up in the fallen leaves that are a salve for my burning feet, but the smell of water keeps me going. Manu isn't at the club today or tomorrow. He isn't in the dressing room, in the living water, in the sun, on the sand, in the big grid of plastic, flesh, lotion, parasols and drinks. Without him, there's only all of that. I don't want to go back, but I don't know where else to go. So I walk, my body leaning toward the ground, zigzagging down the slope that gets steeper and wetter, interrupted by whitish rock surfaces. The protruding roots of the trees make bony stairs. The air gets thicker with a smell of something hidden and fermented. Behind a small mound or a big anthill thirty yards down, a lake appears, dark and glassy. I start running, weaving around the ridge and down the last steep part before the ground flattens into mud and low, crawling plants. I lie down on the rocky shore and drink and cry.

We got drunk and wanted to go clubbing, and Mateo said he knew the perfect spot. Hand in hand with Lasse and Melanie, I followed him down the boulevard. The road was jammed with people heading home from dinner or on their way out for a drink. It was like someone had shifted the gears somewhere in the resort's control room, from the long, sluggish and way-too-bright daytime to the hectic and sensual mood of the night. The bars were playing tropical lounge music, the waiters became overly attentive, the tourists made-up and perfumed. The sun sank and muted the light to a comfortable red glow that made people's tans look healthy and beautiful. I even caught myself wanting all the shining flesh pressing in around me, all the half-naked women and men, to rub up against them on a dance floor or in a hotel room, like it was sex pheromones being sprayed out of the fans in the bar awnings. I wouldn't be surprised if Cancún had some furtive agreement with the northern European negative-birth-rate nations, *Do it for Denmark.*

We continued to the party area at the resort's northernmost point and went into La Vaquita. It was decorated like a strange blend of strip club and theme park: cow-print tables and movie theatre seats, cow-print carpet, dark-red metal handrails leading from the booths to the bar and the dance floor with cages on raised platforms. We paid the thirty dollars for the open bar until 2 a.m. The clientele was varied, most were probably tourists from Western Europe and the US, but a lot of locals too, Mateo said. We had left the dance floor and were sitting on one of the spotted couches against the wall.

'There are too many people staring,' I said, nodding toward the bar where people were hanging out.

Mateo said that he needed a whole lot more to drink before he would dance. But he liked it here, he wanted me to know: the alcohol, the music, the body odour, all the anonymous people around us, to him it was the perfect setting for 'a little life reflection.'

'And what do you think about life then?' I asked.

'I'm happy,' he said.

'And what about Melanie?' I asked, feeling suddenly bold because of the way we were seated, both of us with our eyes on our significant others acting out on the dance floor. I felt like we were brothers and could talk to each other about pretty much anything.

'I think she's happy too,' he said. 'But she misses home. Have you noticed how sometimes her gaze slide away, just kind of disappears, in the middle of a conversation? Or when you're out sightseeing... She's travelled too much.'

'Yeah, but what I actually meant was how do you feel about her? She'll have to go home at some point, won't she?'

He thought about it for a moment before answering. 'You remember tourists in a different way than you remember other people.'

'How about you?' he asked a second later. 'How do you feel about your boyfriend?'

'Good,' I said, 'I'm happy... Lasse can get a little worked up sometimes...'

'Yeah, he seems like the kind of guy who might explode at any minute. Poor tree, huh?'

'But he would never actually hurt anyone!' I looked insistently, and maybe also a little angrily, at Mateo, but couldn't tell whether or not he believed me. 'It's himself he's mad at... Don't tell anyone

I said this, but sometimes he hits himself.'

'Okay,' Mateo said, a little sceptical.

'Like, he just lets loose on his own face, until he can't take it anymore. Like he's trying to exorcise something.'

'But how are you supposed to say anything to him then? I mean, if he gets violent toward himself, when you're having a fight for example, is it when you're fighting that he does that?'

'Yeah, most of the time. Or if I tell him that he hurt my feelings—'

'But then it's impossible to reason with him! How can you even get angry at him then — if you want to?'

Well, fuck you, Mateo, I thought. What did he know about Lasse's shame? In reality, its source wasn't Lasse but me, or at least his awareness of having put me in an uncomfortable situation. Really, shame was social or interpersonal or whatever you want to call it, but somewhere on its way into your body, it cut all ties and ended up seeming like it was all about you, yeah, that's exactly what he did, made everything about him! I was sick of the sympathy I felt for Lasse when he hit himself, I was done with it, he should try to get out of himself for once.

'You know they all hate him at the hotel, right?' Mateo asked when I didn't respond. Something rude and arrogant had entered his voice. Maybe he was drunker than I thought.

'What do you mean?' I asked.

'The receptionists, the cleaning staff, they think he brings bad luck... It's just something about him, his nervous energy, it puts them on edge.'

'What would you know about that?'

'A lot, my friend Cristo is the receptionist at your hotel. Obviously we talk about work.'

'Okay, 'hate' is maybe too strong a word,' he said a moment later, and told me that what was draining, what was, to put it bluntly, destroying the locals of Cancún, was the lack of seasons. Of course, there's the rainy season and the ten days at the end of April when the jellyfish approach the shore to mate, but there's no winter when the tourists stay away and let the locals find themselves.

'But our lovers have found each other,' I said, nodding at the dance floor. Mateo looked indifferently at Lasse and Melanie wriggling around each other laughing, and shut down my attempt to reestablish our connection. Now they were taking turns leaning their heads back and shaking their bodies with closed eyes while fanning each other with their hands. The bar was smoky and full of red beams of light that made their wet faces shine. They danced themselves out, came over and gave us a kiss on the cheek, took a sip of their drinks, left to dance some more and showed up with new friends, and so on for the rest of the night until I couldn't recognise them anymore. The drinks were strong and brought out to us in half-litre cups with plastic lids and straws. I sank deeper into the couch, Mateo became increasingly incoherent. At one point, he started talking to me like we didn't know each other:

'So what do you think of Cancún?' 'Which beach is your favourite?' 'And what about the Mexicans, what do you think of them?'

'They're sweet,' I answered, 'so welcoming!'

'Totally! But also a little too forward sometimes, don't you think? You're walking down the street and there they are, trying to shepherd you into one of their restaurants. You're lying on the beach and they come over to offer you something. Or you're at your hotel, on your balcony, even in your room, and they're just there, somewhere.

But you know what? We're not the ones who are everywhere. It's the tourists…'

And then I didn't get to hear anything else because of Melanie, who fell on top of me and shouted into my ear, 'He's the perfect dance partner, your boyfriend!' I looked up at Lasse trying to pull Mateo onto the dance floor, and asked her why. 'He keeps all the other guys away!'

After Lasse fell asleep, I went out on the balcony. There was no sound of traffic, only a few muted voices and a faint clattering of dishes. I could just make out the distant corner of the terrace where Cristo the receptionist was having a drink with two other men, probably friends keeping him company on the night shift. Had Mateo sat there too? Could he see up into our room? Beneath them, the boulevard stretched for a few miles to either side, a glittering strip of hotels, clubs, tattoo parlours and restaurants in the dark sea. A few hundred yards farther down the beach was the Big Cat Beach Club, where we had met the boy who tricked us into being in his movie. I could sense him like an animal senses another animal in the dark. I went back inside and sat at the little desk, with my back to Lasse in bed, plugged the headphones into his computer and pressed play.

At the end, after trying to inhabit the role, kicking the boy and humiliating him, I looked desperately into the lens and said I wanted to stop. In the five seconds that followed, I could feel Lasse's passive presence behind the camera, his sweat and heavy breathing, a strange, ghostly satisfaction that made him hesitate a little too long before turning it off. Something made me rewind and watch those five seconds over and over again, until finally, I identified what it was: a short glitch that sliced the image into a blurry grid. As if the particles that composed the image moved for a moment in a way that couldn't be read by the computer circuit. It gave me the strange sense that the particles were living their own life and really remembered us, the waves of light that we reflected in exactly that moment, me and the boy and the things around us: the sky, the sea, the streetlamps and the palm trees, the plastic chair and the tiled floor that he was lying on with a dull and distant expression, like a plastic film covering the disgust in his eyes, and my foot in his mouth.

I went online and searched 'beach boy licking tourist feet,' 'young boy pushed around by tourists on balcony,' 'tourists using Mexican boy as a table,' and found a website full of images of young boys in swim trunks. I clicked on one of them and was prompted to log in, was about to give up when Lasse's email address and a password were automatically filled in. He swelled in the bed behind me, his eyes sliding wet over my neck and back. Behind the log-in wall, the videos were waiting. There were clips that resembled mine, but also a few where the boys were alone on the shore with a beach ball or some other toy. It felt like I was lying next to Lasse in bed and couldn't move. As the sun crept up from the ocean and into the room, I watched the videos, one by one. Some of the tourists were more violent toward the boys than others. All of the boys had the same dull expression in their eyes. I found the kid from the Big Cat Beach Club, and later me with my foot in his mouth. But there was only one of me and many of him, maybe twenty or thirty videos.

There's nothing special about the beach because I am a beach boy, there's only longing in the sky and the sea. Bill told me why: he says their deep blue is the light that's spread when the sun's rays hit the atmosphere, light that never arrives to touch me, but fills the distance. He walks across the sand in a series of sober movements, straight-backed and in full control. He knows the weight of each object and the strength needed to lift it: parasol, lotion bottle, towels, drinks; in his hands they all leave the ground at the same speed. The owner sacked two other boys a week after hiring him. Now Manu is gone too, and we run around exhausted, trying to keep the guests in our sections satisfied. I never have the time to stop and look over the big grid, reach for the other boys with my eyes, and when I do they're gone behind a swarm of sun-tanned hands suspended in the air, fanning me over: I take orders and deliver drinks, adjust parasols, apply sunscreen and after-sun, without faking anything for anyone. I understand what Jia means when he says the club is one big economy of the sun: everything that is part of it, from the beach chairs' shining grid to the lotions we offer the guests, is derived from the sun and constitutes its house. When the tourists come and lie in it, they become sunbathers. By now we aren't enough hands for more than two at a time to be someone's personal boy, so we pool our tips and divvy them up at night. And of course I say yes to the extra gigs that come my way: cleaning bits and coffee table bits, dog and cat bits, and in all of them I'm on all fours in front of the tourists who order me around, kick and scold me, in the way the owner has instructed me to instruct them. I miss Manu most of the time. Other times it's just me, early in the morning before the club opens, in the still, glittering water I slip around and play. I find the big red beach ball, lift it over my head and watch the water drip from its underbelly. 'Ooo, there you are, my favourite! So big and round...' I say it with my voice at the very front of my throat, and with a lot of air. 'So much bigger than my head.' I say, 'You're all bloated, you're so tight and smooth,' rubbing it across my belly to make that squeaky plastic sound. Then I wrap my arms around it with a giggle and try to keep myself afloat until it spins me around and throws me off. When I'm standing up again, cuddling the ball, I take the needle out of my pocket underwater. That's the hardest part: separating myself from my arm driving the needle into the ball, from my fear of the pop in my ears and the plastic's pop against my skin; I'm supposed to play with it and fondle and enjoy it till the very end. Not show that I am, with my whole body, afraid of the next second. And when it happens I'm only allowed to say 'oof' and laugh a goofy laugh, not so much as granting the flaccid plastic in the water a look.

After five or six uninterrupted takes, the owner sends me to the changing room. I get to lie down in the living water that soothes my swollen skin for ten minutes before I hear the other boys arrive, and I rush out of the pool. The door opens, and they walk in on a fan of light that disperses them across the bench and folds back together in a golden string along the doorframe.

'You're up early today,' Ginger says, pulling off his jeans.

'I couldn't sleep,' I say, 'just sat by the lagoon until morning.'

'What?' Ginger says. 'I can't even get out of bed these days, and I collapse as soon as I get back home. Everything's so much harder since Bill arrived and made the rest of us unnecessary.'

'It doesn't have anything to do with Bill,' Jia says from the corner. 'Don't you see, this is the owner's way of trying to pin us under the sun. Just like the parasols. He's trying to exhaust us.'

'You and your fucking sun economy,' Ginger says, and turns to me and Bill.

'The owner is trying to lock us up in the house of the sun,' I say, less because I know it's true than to shift the conversation away from Bill, who's breathing nervously at my side. His dry shoulder rubs up and down against mine. He can probably tell that I've been lying in the pool.

'Yeah,' Jia says. 'He doesn't want us to see the sunscreen and after-sun as anything other than before and after the sun, or the guests as more than sunbathers. Or the sun as more than...'

'Fuck the guests,' Ginger says.

'Yeah, fuck the guests. But the parasols...' Jia says, and places a hand on Ginger's inner thigh. '*Para-sol, Para-sun*,' he says, almost sings, in a light voice that's simultaneously playful and powerful, drawing circles between Ginger's legs.

Ginger is about to protest, but falls silent and gives in, leans his head back and thrusts his groin into the bowl Jia is making with his hand. The sun rises and shines through the bamboo wall. A fluorescent orange fog lifts from the pool in front of the bench and turns into jelly on my feet.

'Para-sun.' I say it how Jia said it, and the word takes the shape of a funnel in my mouth. 'But what does it mean?'

'How am I supposed to know?' Jia laughs.

'Do you want to?' I ask Bill, nodding, and he nods too, and I hand him a shrimp shell from the pile we've been collecting under the bench. We make the best of the things that are. Bill and Jia push me and Ginger headfirst into the pool, follow us laughing and feed our assholes with eggs in the living water, while we all sing in chorus: 'Para-sol, Para-sun ...'

When we're done getting dressed, shrimp shells on Bill's and Jia's dicks in our spines soft and transparent with eggs in the sun on the sandy ground, we go down to the beach. The beach chairs, the sand and the parasols are all equally white, shining like a vast blob of sunscreen. The flags with the lion logo droop on their poles along the boulevard. The planks of the boardwalk caress the soles of my feet as I cross them one at a time, smooth with soft furrows. Ginger's hand is flat on Bill's lower back, Bill's hand on mine, and my arm draped over Jia's shoulder, and when we let go and disband I register a heaviness at the base of my back: a sack of eggs, one for each boy, as if in the changing room I absorbed us inside me to avoid having to go through the workday by myself. As Jia and Ginger walk in their boyish rocking swagger toward their respective middle-aged couples farther down the boardwalk, I make my-self harmless and small-hipped in the eyes of the three young, muscular men walking toward me. Bill hangs back to let two Scandinavian women come to him, as if of their own accord. We have to take advantage of these early hours before the club fills up to make some good money.

'Hey, guys, welcome to the club,' I say six feet away with a not-too-humble bow. 'What if I were your personal boy this morning? Shade, sun, sunscreen, drinks and snacks, whatever you need — I'll take care of it?'

'I think we can put our own sunscreen on,' one of them says in a thick American accent.

'But some drinks would be nice...' another says, looking innocently at his friends.

'Well, then, follow me,' I say, showing them to my section. On the way down the boardwalk, we pass Bill, and when he greets the two women with a noble bow, a nervous child breaks through his figure, contorted and attention-seeking. The eggs expand and hatch. I kneel and smooth out three towels on three lounge chairs. The guys order three Long Island iced teas and a bag of peanuts. There's something greedy about the way they recline in the sun in their tiny swim trunks. Their clean-shaven legs hair and chests are bulging. They lather themselves up in tanning oil, Australian Gold, which makes them glisten and lifts them up to the sun, three bronze plates swaying and swelling over the sand.

I shoot steady through the water, propelled by my lower body: its five pairs of paddling legs in constant motion, slightly staggered. It's only a matter of getting started, and then the speed spreads through my joints until they feel like one big buzzing organism that's both mine and foreign, and my tail fan works like a rudder. The other boys swim up alongside me, appearing at the edge of my panorama: three grey-brown, almost transparent shrimp with serrated rostrums and dark-red eyes on stalks. We swim across the bare sandy bottom, away from the coast where the water is full to the brim with light and perforated by human legs. A shadow is cast like a solar eclipse by someone in a swim tube. An imbalance, something bitter and sour and foreign in the water, makes me close my mouth and block my gills. I flash a yellow, jagged pattern down my back, see a veil of sunscreen hanging off the body in the swim ring and go faster. Finally away from the bitterness, I pump water through my gills and feel the oxygen spread its clarity through my body. Our paddling legs propel us farther along the seafloor, into the depths of low seaweed and seagrass. Beneath the big, bowed leaves, all the light disappears in the water, but I'm not alone; the distance to the bottom, the other shrimp boys, the movements in the water and its chemical composition, it all makes itself felt through my antennae: it is also under my shell. The middle of it stiffens into a slightly thicker carapace that connects my head and my upper body and ends between my eyes in a horned snout.

At the zenith we're all really busy, everyone wants water and breezes and sunscreen for their bodies. Even the three Americans, who have been meticulously oiling up and changing position every hour for maximum exposure, want to be shielded and have their parasols put up. 'Sure you don't want me to do it for you?' I ask as they're futilely grasping at their backs. 'For a little extra money?' When I add that they must be sore from all that working out — don't they deserve a little massage? — it's like they finally get the attention they've been waiting for; in any case they turn into supple, willing flesh in my hands and tell me all about their workout routine. Meanwhile, I notice a young woman standing up by the entrance, staring at me. I can't see her face from here, only that it's turned towards me, that her whole body is. For five or ten seconds she stands there, on the verge of coming down here, and then it's like she changes her mind; the tension leaves her body and mine. A freight ship honks out on the ocean behind me. She turns around and gets into a cab that swings out and slides into the shimmering traffic —

On my way to get drinks for the guys, I look out over the club and suddenly can't help but laugh at all the things I hate: the sun-bleached boardwalk that stretches from the reception desk to the beach chairs; the beach chairs that hold a little time in their big vibrating grid and fix the sun in the zenith; the guests greedily soaking up the sun, offering themselves without reserve, wanting its rays all over them, only to block it out by any means possible: fans and broad-brimmed hats, water bottles, parasols, protective and cooling salves, soothing remedies for a cult that worships a sun that will soon leave them, or receive them. All the things here are ridiculous without the sun. Shadowless objects under the open sky, translucent and relegated to a dim life on the sand, in the skin, under the sea.

With my tail fan I steer slowly toward a rock of moulted shells between dull corals: furry grey columns, a hard pale-yellow brain, sponges with soft folds and stony skeletons. Each coral is a colony of polyps. They pull their skeletons out of the water, grow them over many generations, surrender them to the big communal skeleton when they die. I catch the bottom with my legs, the thin sticks that dangle when I swim. A complex, organic taste of food and danger excites me. Our eyes rolling in semicircles, we wander across calcified limestone, keeping an eye out for crevices where molluscs might suddenly emerge with their tentacles.

Finally we reach the cleaning station. Ginger and Bill position themselves on the protrusion between two copper-red stone corals, flash a row of violet stripes down their backs and wave their antennae from side to side. The reef is pale with scattered dull colours, the corals stressed by the acidic water. Two large, eel-like fish swim toward us and settle with open mouths in front of Ginger and Bill, who get started on one of them. The other seems a little uneasy, so me and Jia stroke it with our antennae before we start to clean its teeth and oral cavity. With our front legs, we scrape them clean of food particles and eat whatever tastes good. Then we float around on our backs for a bit, Jia's legs around my neck, and look up at the vaulted darkness speckled by teeth.

It's nice and warm here, nothing to fear in this fish's mouth. Every once in a while, its jaw snaps and the light disappears, but we come out whole and keep cleaning. We smell and taste our way to the dead tissue and parasites in its skin.

A little later, in the middle of cleaning a set of greasy gills, I feel a tight, skeletal sensation in my flesh, a growing stiffness travelling through my back and abdomen. A sense of something important that's going to happen on the beach. My shell softens, the light is fading. It flickers through the water in dim, crooked rays that don't really reach me.

When we were done getting dressed, our shells on dicks ribbed and prickling in spines of jelly on the sandy ground, we went down to the beach carrying buckets of living water. Black sky and sand illuminated by the reddish glow of the beach chairs, which had absorbed the sun's rays in their grid-work. In the sand we dug a circular basin a little larger than a parasol and filled it up with living water: dim orange, viscous, full of milky eggs with veins. It was steaming in the cool air. Around the basin we planted four parasols upside down in the sand, twisting them down into the viscous layers. The shafts protruding a hand's length above the sand, we greased them with after-sun before we lowered ourselves to straddle them. We threw a beach chair into the basin and sang:

After the sun, after the sun / things are beside themselves / quiet, futile, set free / into the unknown life we're asking about / Why does the vulture always start with the eyes? / Which sides of you didn't we see / beach chair, after-sun, Para-sun / making the best of the things that are / after the sun, after the sun ...

Dawn is coming: a dim light-blue shimmer that merges with the earth's shadow, the dark sky. The earth is turning a new side to the sun, but slowly, reluctantly, doubting. It isn't morning.

My eyes can't make out the feet in the sand, the backs in front of me, the sand from the water from the sky. Or whatever the landscape might be to our left. We listen to the sea and walk north. Me and Jia and Ginger and Bill, and lots of other boys from the beach clubs we've passed through. We carry a beach chair, some after-sun and a parasol, the way that they emerged from the living water, a little beside themselves. We tell each other what happened on the beach:

The beach chair sank a few inches and was caught by the living water. Rocking on our shafts we sang for hours. And when the after-sun and our secretions ran dry, the pain and the blood started to run. The water became warmer, the surface pearled. The beach chair flickered and blurred in the basin. We could no longer tell our own voices from one another's assholes from the hole deeper inside us that the pain and the foreign blood ran down the hollow parasol shafts softening the sandy soil beneath the basin. A pool of colour whirled at our knees.

Puru-sol, Para-sun / luminous funnel in my mouth / my gut, my earth / makes the next of the things that are / without the sun, in a house without a master / things that were / become nothing / in Para-sun, Para-sun ...

'Listen,' someone says up in front, and makes everyone stop to listen. From the sea, rippling through the water and up to the beach, comes a continuous sound like a foghorn, combined with deep grunting, and once in a while an even deeper, rising 'ba-ba-ba-ba-ba-ba...' 'It's the fish ringing in the dawn,' another says. 'They see the light before we do because they're deeper, deep down.'

The water lit up and changed from blood red to violet to orange with belts of white. A slimy fog in the same colours rose from it and condensed in the vague outline of a beach chair with a web of veins. In the mist around it, transparent images lit up for a second and blurred: corpses of tourists sinking into hotel beds with jellyfish and crabs, compacted and pressed into a thick, dark-brown fluid... sinking through the hotel's skeleton and running out and stiffening in solid shapes on each floor: shampoo bottle, hair dryer, fan. On the beach, a cave of beach chairs, swelling red with the warmth of a fire or the warmth of the earth's core. The owner of the club is sitting in a hidden room above the reception desk, watching everything that happens on the beach. A thick cable is plugged into his neck, which converts our movements into light that's spread across thousands of white faces with sweat on their upper lips...

Now the horizon is almost visible, the sea a bit greyer than the sky. The blue light spread through the atmosphere stretches its tentacles down and draws out the contours of the things before us: a few trees and bushes in bony terrain, maybe some rocks. Fleeting legs, shoulders and the back of a head walking in front of me. I'm hungry, but don't feel like eating in this light that doesn't hide the stars. Dawn is coming. A morning before morning, a night before night. The time of the fish, the lizards and the felines. They slither across the earth, rustling in sand and shrubbery.

We threw a bottle of after-sun into the basin and sang. It rose in a slimy fog and breathed: spitting its contents out in little squirts, releasing the pressure and recovering its shape. In the water, after-sun sprawled into rippled images:

people in the desert luring the sun with lotion in large pools. Lizards and succulents and crawling humans digging through layers of earth. A choreographed dance on a public square. A child stands in the middle of a group of older, more experienced dancers, watches their movements and copies them a bit out of sync... takes a step forward and gives over fully and nervously to each step, takes a step back and waits for the next. In the intervening beats, the child looks like a remnant of itself, a potential unaltered by the attempt to learn the new customs of the planet on which it's arrived.

We walk along the water, over rocks and sand, past the ruins of small fisheries, ruined hotels and jetties, large parabolas that the ocean has eaten away. That's how it looks in the gentle light. Dawn is coming in the soil now, orange and dusty. It oozes out, some places thicker than others, slithering along the sand and the rocks and finding itself. It doesn't hurt to look at, because you can only look in it, and looking in that light is more like eating. It doesn't make things disappear. They linger in their outlines like a promise of themselves and something to come. My lips are cold and cracked, my muscles sore. But deeper inside, at the base of my abdomen and close to my spine, there's something that hurts in a different way. It's accumulated inside me at the beach club, during the video recordings, under the sun. It is dawning now: a weak orange light in my asshole, just like it's dawning in the other boys and in the things, binding us together in a web that's still dim. One day, it will lead to something.

We threw a parasol into the basin and sang. A slimy fog rose from it and condensed in a long, hollow shaft and a fabric full of flickering images: fire spreading through the club, through towels and parasols, a flaming grid seen from above. We use a huge towel to contain the smoke and release it in shifting intervals, a hazy code... A low, crawling forest where the trees bend and curl toward the ground, pressing their crowns into the soil. In the twilight, parasols with their fabric stretched inside out make funnels that catch the rain and lead into big pools full of seaweed and crustaceans. In the water a deep orange light. It's led through grooves between the trees and illuminates the first few feet above the ground... All the while we focused on singing the words, on saying them just to hear them in our mouths, to make room for their moisture, their hardness, their flickering unfolding: *Para-sun, Para-sun*, that was our prayer: an emission of sound waves in the right frequency, waves that made the living water oscillate. And when the thing rose, suspended above the basin in slimy fog, we tried to sing in a way that would resonate with it. When the word grasped the thing, the thing took the word onto itself and into the water with a splash.

The sky slips into a darker blue, black at the edges. The beach arcs red in the west. We follow it until we come to a cape where we can see out over the ocean to both sides. It's bulging with Para-sun that drives the blue out of the sky. The yellow along the horizon fades. Everywhere the earth flares up in a mild, orange light that traces its slope in the black morning. 'Come, let's go inland.'

ACKNOWLEDGEMENTS

A thank-you from the heart to everyone who read and cared for this book as I wrote it. A special thanks to: Andreas Amdy Eckhardt-Læssøe, Rolf Sparre Johansson, Anita Beikpour, Stinne Eika Rasmussen, Pejk Malinovski and Forlaget Basilisk.

A number of writers and artists helped inspire the stories in this book — some of their sentences and images are hiding under mine — Chris Marker, Clarice Lispector, Eileen Myles, Lars Norén, Paul the Apostle, Simone Weil, William Burroughs and Roberto Bolaño.

Graphic design by Kasper Vang
Printed and bound by KOPA, Lithuania, 2021
First edition, 2021

A CIP catalogue record for this book is available from the British Library
ISBN 978-1-9999928-5-9

Lolli Editions
132 Defoe House, Barbican
London EC2Y 8ND
United Kingdom
www.lollieditions.com